THE Berenstain BEAR SCOUTS TREASURY

ISBN 0-439-26507-X

12 11 10 9 8 7 6 5 4 3 2 1   0 1 2 3 4 5 6/0

Printed in the U.S.A.   23

First Scholastic printing, August 2000

THE Berenstain BEAR SCOUTS TREASURY

by Stan & Jan Berenstain
Illustrated by Michael Berenstain

Scholastic Inc.
New York   Toronto   London   Auckland   Sydney
Mexico City   New Delhi   Hong Kong

This treasury includes:

*The Berenstain Bear Scouts
in Giant Bat Cave*

*The Berenstain Bear Scouts
and the Humongous Pumpkin*

The Berenstain Bear Scouts Meet Bigpaw

*The Berenstain Bear Scouts
Save That Backscratcher*

THE Berenstain BEAR SCOUTS

in

Giant Bat Cave

THE Berenstain BEAR SCOUTS

in

Giant Bat Cave

by Stan & Jan Berenstain
Illustrated by Michael Berenstain

• Table of Contents •

• Chapter 1 •

One for All, and All for One

The Bear Scouts met with Scout Leader Jane about once a month. They usually met on merit badge business. That's what today's meeting was about.

"We've decided to try for the Good Government Merit Badge, Scout Leader," said Scout Brother.

"Goo goo," said Sister.

"I should know better than to ask," said Jane, "but why are you talking baby talk?"

The troop grinned.

"That's slang for 'good government,'" said Scout Fred.

Scout Leader Jane almost smiled, but kept herself from doing so. The troop liked to make jokes. Especially Scout Sister, who was a bit of a smarty. But Jane thought it best to be serious. She was not only a scout leader, she was a teacher at Bear Country School as well.

In fact, both Scout Sister and Scout Lizzy were in her class. The other two members of the troop were Scout Brother and Scout Fred. They were two grades ahead of Sister and Lizzy.

But girl or boy, younger or older, they were all scouts together. "One for all, and all for one" was their slogan. It came from a book Scout Fred had read—it was called *The Bear Musketeers*. It told about some soldiers from olden times. They would cross their swords and shout, "One for all, and all for one!" Then they would rush off to rescue a princess or slay a dragon. There weren't any princesses in Bear

Country, or any dragons—at least as far as anyone knew.

Nor did the Bear Scouts have swords to cross. But they crossed other things when they said their slogan—like straws one time when they were having milkshakes at the Burger Bear, or rulers or pencils at school, or even sticks when they were gathering wood for a campfire.

Brother, Sister, Fred, and Lizzy liked being Bear Scouts. They liked having Jane as their leader, too. One of the reasons was that she trusted them. The scouts knew that other scout leaders fussed about everything their troops wanted to do. But not Jane. She didn't even know where the troop's secret clubhouse was. The only person besides the scouts who did know was Farmer Ben. That was because the scouts' secret clubhouse was an old chicken coop that Farmer Ben wasn't using for chickens anymore.

From the outside it still looked like a broken-down old chicken coop. It looked much better from the inside. It wasn't fancy. There wasn't much furniture, and what there was was very simple. The table was an old door that rested on sawhorses. There were two old kitchen chairs that Farmer Ben had given them. But mostly the scouts sat in the small grandstand

they had made from the chicken roost.
They had done this by nailing boards to
the poles that the chickens had roosted
upon.

The scouts had been able to keep their
clubhouse secret because nobody ever saw
them going into it. Farmer Ben had built
the chicken coop onto an old hollow tree.
The scouts went in through the hollow
tree. There were bushes around the open-
ing, so the scouts were able to slip in without ever being seen.

It hadn't been easy turning the chicken
coop into a clubhouse. The scouts had been
very happy when Farmer Ben told them
they could have the place. But when they
first went in, they were shocked. It was
the dirtiest place any of them had ever
seen—and the smelliest! At first they
couldn't stop yelling "Pew!" over and over
again. Their eyes teared and their noses
burned. But they rolled up their sleeves

and went to work. They carried out bag
after bag of chicken feathers. They
scrubbed and scrubbed and scrubbed.
After a lot of cleaning up and fixing up,
the place began to look like a real clubhouse.

You'd hardly know that it had once
been a chicken coop, except for two things:
It still had a funny smell on rainy days,
and once in a while a chicken would show
up and make itself at home.

• Chapter 2 •

The Honor Wall

One wall of the Bear Scouts' clubhouse
was special. They called it their honor
wall. On it were the merit badges the
troop had already earned. There were
three of them: a Good Deed Merit Badge,
a Water Safety Merit Badge, and a
Recycling Merit Badge.

They had earned the first by helping
the Widder McGrizz when she was ill with
the flu. They had done her grocery shop-
ping and other helpful things. They had
earned the second by learning the dead
bear's float, the doggie paddle, and the

sidestroke. They had earned the third
merit badge by putting paper, glass, and
metal in different cans for trash pickup.

The three merit badges were pinned to
a ribbon that was tacked to the honor
wall. It was a long ribbon. There was
room on it for more merit badges.

But the most important thing on the honor wall was the Bear Scout Oath. This is what it looked like, and this is what it said.

THE BEAR SCOUT OATH

A Bear Scout...
Is as honest as the day is long.
Admits when he or she is wrong.
Respects the creatures of creation.
Views TV in moderation.
Is never cruel, rude, or mean.
Plays the game fair and clean.
Does his or her best at school.
Following the golden rule,
    always respects the rights of
        others,
    including even sisters' and brothers.'

Signed:
    Scout Brother
    ❀Scout Sister❀
    —Scout Fred—
    Scout Lizzy

• Chapter 3 •

A Letter for Gus

The Bear Scout Oath hung on the wall of
Scout Leader Jane's office as well. It was
exactly the same, except for one thing.
There were five names at the bottom
instead of four. The fifth name was that of
Scout Leader Jane.

Jane was proud of her troop. One of the
things she was most proud of was the way
they did things on their own. Take merit
badges, for instance. They got them the
old-fashioned way: They *earned* them.

Leader Jane got up from her desk and
took a book from the shelves. It was the
Official Bear Scout Handbook. "Hmm,"
she said. "Let's see what you have to do to

11

earn the Good Government Merit Badge." Jane read aloud, "The Good Government Badge can be earned in a number of ways: one, by studying the workings of government; two, by helping during an election; three, by interviewing at least three important government officials. The troop will then report to the troop leader. The leader will decide whether or not to award the Good Government Merit Badge."

The scouts thought it over. They couldn't choose "helping during an election" because it wasn't election time. They couldn't interview three important government officials because Beartown didn't have three important officials. It had only two: Mayor Horace J. Honeypot and Chief of Police Bruno.

"I guess studying the workings of government is all that's left," said Scout Sister. "But how are we going to do that?"

"You will do that by going to an important meeting at Town Hall this evening," said Jane. She took a piece of Bear Scout letter paper and began writing.

"Say, wait a minute," said Scout Fred. "I know about that meeting. My parents are going to it. But they couldn't find a sitter because everybody else is going to that meeting, too."

"Our parents were having the same problem," said Scout Brother.

"Mine too," said Scout Lizzy.

"Well," said Jane, "they won't need sitters, because you'll be going, too. They don't usually allow cubs at town meetings. So here's a letter telling Gus the doorkeeper to let you in. He was in my class when he was a cub. He knows better than to not do what I say."

"Leader Jane?" said Sister.

"Yes, Scout Sister."

"What's this big important meeting about?"

"You'll find that out soon enough," said Jane.

• Chapter 4 •

No Cubs Allowed

The Bear Scouts had never seen such a crowd. Everybody who was anybody was going into the meeting. Everybody except cubs, of course. The Bear Scouts were the only cubs in sight.

"Gee," said Lizzy, "I hope they let us in."

"This letter from Scout Leader Jane should do it," said Brother. But he was just as nervous as Lizzy. Their parents had already gone into the meeting. So had Brother and Sister's grandparents.

"Just a minute, please. Where do you think you're going? This is a meeting for grown-ups."

It was Gus, the doorkeeper. He was so big that the scouts could hardly see past him into the auditorium.

"W-well," said Brother, "we're trying for our Good Government Merit Badges and ..."

"Show him the letter," said Sister.

The letter was short and to the point. It said, "To Whom It May Concern — especially Gus the doorkeeper, who used to be in my class. Please admit my Bear Scout troop. They are on official business." It was signed "Scout Leader Jane."

"Well, I don't know," said Gus, reading the letter. The bears lined up outside began to shout, "Let us in!" and "What's the holdup?"

"What beems to see the bubble, Gus? Er — what seems to be the trouble?"

It was the voice of Mayor Horace J. Honeypot himself. It was easy to tell because Mayor Honeypot often got the fronts and the backs of his words mixed up.

Mayor Honeypot took the letter from Gus and read it. "Let them in, my all beans — er, by all means! Why, bubs — er, cubs — are our country's future!"

The scouts did not like all the fuss. They quickly found seats in the back row of the crowded auditorium.

"You know, we still don't know what this big important meeting is about," said Fred.

"That may be," said Sister. "But I'll tell you this: It's got to be about something a little strange. Because *look*!" She pointed to the stage.

"Good grief!" said Brother. "Ralph Ripoff! Right up there on the stage! And shaking hands with the mayor!"

The scouts really couldn't be blamed for being surprised, even shocked. Ralph was famous around Beartown. A better word would be "infamous," which means famous in a bad way. The kindest thing to be said about Ralph was that he couldn't exactly be trusted. A not-so-kind thing to

17

say was that Ralph was a no-good, low-down crook.

Maybe the best way to tell about Ralph Ripoff is to repeat what some of his fellow bears said about him.

Here's what Grizzly Gramps, Brother and Sister's grandfather, had to say: "Ralph reminds me of one of those hot-air balloons: no visible means of support — except the hot air he's full of."

Papa had a different idea about Ralph: "I like Ralph. Sure, he's smooth and tricky. You just have to watch him, that's all."

This is what Mama had to say about Ralph: "I was taught that if you couldn't say something good about someone, you shouldn't say anything. So I won't say anything."

• Chapter 5 •

Something Wonderful

But no matter what Gramps, Papa, and Mama thought about Ralph, there he was up there on the stage. He and the mayor were shaking hands like old friends.

The mayor tested the sound system. "One-two, one-two," he said. As he did so, a big movie screen came down behind him.

"I wid you all belcome—er, bid you all welcome!" said the mayor. "I have called this cheating—er, meeting—to talk about a wonderful new project. And now, leading citizen, Mr. Ralph Ripoff . . ."

"Leading citizen?" whispered Scout Brother.

"Doesn't he mean *leading crook*?" whispered Scout Sister.

". . . will sell you—er, tell you—about something that will be a great boon to Beartown . . ."

"What's 'boon'?" whispered Sister.

"*Boon,*" whispered Fred, who read the dictionary for fun. "*Something good, something of value.*"

". . . something that will bring much happiness to the citizens of Beartown. And something," the mayor went on, "that will also bring *much money* to the citizens of Beartown."

There was a buzz in the audience when they heard the word "money."

"And so it is with much pleasure that I give you my great and good friend, Mr. Rip Ralphoff—er, Ralph Ripoff!"

As Ralph stood up, the lights went down. A spotlight shone on Ralph. He clicked a clicker and said, "First slide, please."

A picture filled the screen. It was a picture of a place everybody knew about.

"It's Giant Bat Cave!" said Scout Fred.

"Why is he showing us a picture of that yucky place?" said Sister. Others in the auditorium were wondering the same thing.

"That's right," said Ralph. "It's Giant Bat Cave. A nasty, filthy place if ever there was one. Filled with thousands of nasty, filthy bats."

As Ralph spoke he clicked his clicker and more pictures came onto the screen. There was a picture of the cave with a thick cloud of bats pouring out of its mouth.

"Ooh!" said Sister. "Bats give me the shivers."

There was a picture of what could have been the inside of a great dragon's mouth with rows and rows of terrible teeth. Of course, it wasn't. It was the inside of Giant Bat Cave, and the "teeth" were stalactites and stalagmites.

"And now," said Ralph, "Ripoff Productions presents ... *something wonderful*! New slide, please!"

When the next slide came on the screen, the crowd couldn't believe its eyes. It showed the outside of Giant Bat Cave, but it wasn't spooky and gloomy anymore. It was bright and beautiful. There was a great golden sign that said WELCOME TO RALPH'S CAVERAMA — THE UNDERGROUND WONDERLAND.

The next picture showed the inside. It was even more beautiful. It no longer looked like a dragon's mouth with terrible teeth. It looked like ... well, *an underground wonderland*! There were colored lights, all kinds of fun rides, and more gift shops and food stands than you could count.

• Chapter 6 •

All Those in Favor, Say "Aye!"

At first a hush came over the crowd. As the lights came up, so did the crowd. They stood as one and cheered and cheered. The Bear Scouts joined in. Except for Scout Lizzy, who was *not* standing or cheering.

"What a great idea!" shouted Brother. "An underground theme park!"

Getting cheered was a new thing for Ralph. He was more used to getting chased down the road by folks he had tricked or cheated. Ralph liked being cheered. He smiled and raised his hands over his head.

Mayor Honeypot looked very pleased

too. He held out his hands to shush the crowd. "Now, before putting this to a vote," he said, "the law says we have to take comments. Yes, Squire Grizzly. Do you have a comment?"

Squire Grizzly was Beartown's richest citizen. He owned supermarkets, gas stations, a bank, and a TV station.

"I think Mr. Ripoff's project is a good idea," said the Squire. "It will bring visitors from all over Bear Country. It will be very good for business. Lady Grizzly and I will vote 'yes.'"

Many leading citizens spoke in favor of Ralph's project. Max Bearskin, owner of the Bearskin Arms Motel, thought it was a fine idea. "It will keep my motel rooms filled all year round," he said.

Brad Bruin of Bruin, Bruin, Bruin, and Grizzly, Beartown's leading law firm, offered to draw up the legal papers — for a fee, of course.

The audience was excited about Ralph's

project. Papa Bear, who was a woodwork-
er, was very excited. He turned to Mama
and said, "See, I told you Ralph wasn't
such a bad guy. That Caverama's going to
need a lot of woodwork."

"Perhaps," said Mama, "Ralph will let
us put in a little quilt shop." Mama's quilt-
ing club raised money for Beartown
Hospital.

"Of course he will," said Papa. "I'll
speak to him about it."

"Maybe I could put in a vegetable
stand!" said Farmer Ben.

Grizzly Gramps had a very different
idea about Ralph's project. "I can't stand
this any longer," he said. "Somebody's got
to warn these folks. The only one that's
gonna make money out of Ralph's
Caverama is Ralph. Ripoff's his name, and
rippin' folks off is his game. So I gotta
speak my mind." He started to stand to
have his say, but Gran stopped him.

"Hush up, you old grouch!" said Gran.

Her hobby was reading palms and telling fortunes. "Maybe Ralph will let me set up a little fortune-telling booth."

Grizzly Gramps just groaned.

Just about everybody, except Gramps, was talking about some way of being a part of Ralph's Caverama. But nobody at that meeting had given a single thought to what might happen to the thousands of bats when their home was turned into an underground theme park. Nobody, that is, except Bear Scout Lizzy.

"All right. Let's quiet down now," said the mayor. "It's vime for a tote — er, time for a vote. All those in favor of turning Giant Bat Cave into a wonderful money-making underground theme park, raise your hands and say 'aye!'"

Hundreds of hands shot up. The shouts of "aye!" shook the building.

Mayor Honeypot looked out over the sea of raised hands. It was almost like counting votes in the next election.

"All right," said the mayor. "There's really no need to bother, but by law I have to ask all those opposed to raise their hands and say 'nay!'"

A single "nay!" sounded in the auditorium. It was a small voice, but it could be heard clearly in the silence. But whose voice was it? It couldn't be Grampa's.

Everybody looked around. But they couldn't see the naysayer.

So that she could be seen, Bear Scout Lizzy stood on her chair and said it again. "Nay!" she said loud and clear.

Scouts Brother, Sister, and Fred looked at Lizzy. They were just as surprised as everybody else.

Mayor Honeypot was surprised and

very annoyed. He looked out into the auditorium. "Why, as I live and breathe, it's a bub — er, cub. Who let that bub — er, cub — in here?"

"You did, Mr. Mayor," said Gus, the doorkeeper.

"Well, don't let it happen again," said the mayor. "As for you, young lady, you're a bub — er, cub. And cubs don't vote!"

"That may be, sir," said Lizzy in a small but strong voice. "But somebody has to speak for the bats. They will be homeless if you . . ."

"All right, you cubs, out of here!" said Gus. He pushed them out the door.

• Chapter 7 •

Nature's Creatures, Great and Small

Scouts Brother, Sister, and Fred shouldn't have been surprised when Lizzy stood up for the bats. They knew that Lizzy had a special feeling for animals. "Nature's creatures, great and small, nature's creatures, one and all" was a favorite saying of Lizzy's. It told how she felt about animals.

While the members of the Bear Scout troop were "one for all and all for one," each scout was his or her own person with his or her own special talents. Brother was pretty much of a straight arrow and a natural leader. Scout Sister had lots of spunk.

Scout Fred was smart as a whip. And Scout Lizzy had this amazing way with animals—all kinds of animals. Butterflies would light on her finger. Squirrels would bring her acorns. Lizzy could even pet a skunk without getting skunked.

But her fellow scouts didn't know she had a thing for bats. Now they had upset the mayor and gotten themselves kicked out of a big important meeting. How would they earn their Good Government Merit Badges now?

The scouts were talking about it as they walked home.

"Look, Lizzy," said Sister, "butterflies, squirrels, even skunks are one thing—but bats! Yuck!"

Lizzy didn't say anything. But as they walked along in the evening, she held up her hand. Fireflies began to land on it. After a while Lizzy's hand was almost like a lamp lighting their way.

"Well, I for one think Lizzy's got a point," said Fred. "Those bats have lived in

Giant Bat Cave for hundreds, even thousands, of years."

"Sure," said Sister, "but Ralph's Caverama looked really cool. And besides, you heard what he said. How bats are filthy and all."

"I happen to know that's not true," said Fred. "They're not filthy. They're at least as clean as Ralph."

"Maybe so," said Sister, "but they *are* weird. I mean, they like to hang upside down."

"What's the harm in that?" said Fred. "Being against somebody just because they like to hang upside down is plain prejudice."

"I guess so," said Sister. "What do you think, Brother?"

Brother didn't answer. He just walked along deep in thought.

"Good-bye, little friends," said Lizzy. She held up her glowing hand. Her firefly friends flew off in every direction. Then

Lizzy turned to her fellow scouts. "Dirty or clean, upside down or right side up," she said, "taking away the bats' home is totally, totally wrong. And we have to stop it from happening. What *do* you think, Brother?"

"I agree with you," said Brother. "The trouble is, bats don't vote."

"Maybe bats don't vote," said Fred. "But they do something just as important. They eat bugs. Zillions of 'em. Why, if it weren't for bats ... "

"Say, that's right," said Brother. "Sure, it's all part of the ecology. What do you say we take this problem to Professor Actual Factual over at the Bearsonian?"

"It's a deal," said Fred. "We'll go over there first thing in the morning."

That's when they heard someone shouting. "Hey! Wait for me!"

It was Grizzly Gramps. The scouts slowed down so Gramps could catch up.

• Chapter 8 •

Gramps Remembers

"Hi, Gramps," said the scouts.

"Hi. I sure was proud of you cubs back there standin' up to Ralph and the mayor. Ralph's got folks' tongues hangin' out for all that money. It's like old J. P. Bearnum said: There's a sucker born every minute. And Ralph had a whole town hall full of 'em back there."

"Gramps, we were just talking about how important bats are to the ecology," said Brother. "Do you have any idea how Ralph can be stopped?"

"Well," said Gramps, "I'm not much of an *e*-cologist. I'm more of a *Ralph*-ologist. I think the only way to stop Ralph is to beat him at his own game. You've got to trick him, fool him, *scare him off.*"

Gramps looked back. Gran and the scouts' parents were catching up. "Now, listen carefully," said Gramps. "When I was a cub I used to play around that cave. Pretty scary place. We had a little rhyme we used to say.

"Giant Bat Cave
Of Beartown fame
Has the word 'giant'
In its name.
Giant Bat Cave ...
Think about that.
Which is the giant,
The cave or the bat?"

The scouts looked at Gramps. What was he trying to tell them?

"Are you trying to tell us that there's some kind of giant monster bat living in that cave?" said Sister.

"Not tryin' to tell you anything," said Gramps. "Just sayin' a little rhyme we

used to say when we were cubs. Just
remember that last part:

> "Giant Bat Cave ...
> Think about that.
> Which is the giant,
> the cave or *the bat*?"

Grizzly Gran caught up and took
Gramps by the arm. "Come on, Gramps.
You ought to be ashamed of yourself,
putting ideas into cubs' heads."

"Best place for ideas," said Gramps,
"inside cubs' heads." Gramps called back
over his shoulder. "Mind what I say, now.
Is it the cave that's giant? Or ... is it the
bat?"

The scouts waited for their parents to
catch up. As they all headed home, the
Bear Scouts shared a single thought: If
there really were a giant monster bat in
Giant Bat Cave, Ralph's scheme would be
stopped in its tracks.

• Chapter 9 •
Visiting the Professor

The Bearsonian Institution looked like a cross between a fortress and a castle. But it wasn't either. It was a museum. It was Bear Country's most important museum. Its chief, Professor Actual Factual, was Bear Country's most important scientist.

Actual Factual was the kind of scientist who was interested in everything. He studied plants and animals. He studied the earth, the solar system, and the stars. He was also the kind of scientist who went places and did things. He scuba-dived, dug up dinosaur bones, rock-climbed, and invented things. And all the while he was going and doing, *he was thinking*. That's the key to science: going, doing, and *thinking*.

The professor had helped the Bear Scouts many times before. They had high hopes that he would be able to help them with the problem of Giant Bat Cave.

But there was a sign hanging on the knob of the museum's door. In big letters it said, THE PROFESSOR IS OUT! In smaller letters it said, BE BACK SOON. Then in very small letters it said, WATCH THE SKIES.

What the heck did that mean?

"I think I heard something," said Lizzy, who had extra-special good hearing. She said she could hear a mosquito a block away around the corner — and maybe she could.

Fred took off his glasses and looked up at the sky. Fred wore glasses because he was farsighted. That meant he could see things very far away.

"I think I see what Lizzy hears," he
said. "It's not a bird. It's not exactly a
plane. Why, it's Actual Factual!"
And sure enough it was.

Professor Actual Factual landed right in front of the museum. "Happy to see you, my friends!" he shouted. "What do you think of my miniplane? It's my latest invention!"

The scouts thought it was great. They crowded around the tiny plane. It looked almost like an easy chair with wings, a tail, and a motor.

"That's an old washing machine motor. It worked very well," the professor said proudly. "There's only one problem. My washing machine doesn't work very well now.

"In any case, welcome!" said the professor. "My good friends the Bear Scouts are always welcome at the Bearsonian. And how is your lovely leader, Scout Leader Jane?"

"She's fine, Professor," said Brother as they walked through the museum's lobby. "But this isn't just a visit. We're here about a problem."

The Bear Scouts told Actual Factual the whole Giant Bat Cave story as he led them through the museum. They told why they had gone to the big town hall meeting. They told about Ralph's plan to turn Giant Bat Cave into an underground theme park. They told about how they were worried about the bats that had lived in Giant Bat Cave for thousands of years.

The professor spoke not a word as they walked through the museum. They went through the Hall of Flight, where famous aircraft of Bear Country history were on view. They went through the Hall of Dinosaurs, where the great fossil skeletons were to be seen. Two prize skeletons were those of a Tyrannosaurus rex and a pteranodon, a large flying dinosaur. They went through the Hall of Energy, where the professor had built a huge Tesla Coil, which is a kind of lightning machine. The Bear Scouts had been to the museum many times before, of course. But every

time they came they were filled with the
wonder of science and nature.

Actual Factual unlocked the door of his
office and invited the Bear Scouts in. It
was an amazing place in its own right. It
was packed with books. There were blue-
prints tacked to the walls. There were

models of all kinds. There was a blackboard that was covered with numbers.

Actual Factual sat at his cluttered
desk. He had listened to the whole story
without saying a single word. The scouts
were beginning to wonder if he had been
listening.

"Gee, Professor," said Brother. "What do
you think? We think it's serious."

Actual Factual got up and walked to
the blackboard. He erased all the numbers
and wrote on the blackboard in big bold
letters:

OPERATION:
SAVE THE CAVE

• Chapter 10 •

Worse Than Serious

"It's worse than serious," he said. "It's an apocalypse!"

"Apoca-what?" said Sister.

"Definition, please," said the professor.

"*Apocalypse*: pronounced a-poc-a-lips," said Fred. "*Doom, total disaster.*"

"Thank you, Fred," said the professor. "But let me explain. In the first place, bats have lived in Giant Bat Cave not for thousands of years but for sixty million years. For that whole time they have been an important part of the balance of nature. What makes bats so important is that they eat lots of insects. Bats control insects better than anything else on earth."

"Better than birds?" said Brother.

"Better than frogs?" said Lizzy.

"Better than flyswatters?" said Sister.

"Better than all those put together," said the professor. "Bats eat tons and tons of insects."

"But, Professor," said Sister, "how could there be tons of anything as small as insects?"

"They make up in numbers what they lack in size," said the professor. He went to a globe in the corner of his office. "Just think about this. If you took all the land creatures on the earth and put them on one side of a scale. Then you took all the insects of the earth and put them on the other side of the scale. It's the side with the insects that would weigh more."

"Wow!" said the scouts.

"Now what does that say to you?" asked the professor.

"It says," said Sister, "that if we don't save the cave, we're all gonna get a lot more mosquito bites."

"That's one way of looking at it," said the professor. "Come, scouts. We've got things to attend to if we're going to save the cave."

"Where are we going?" asked Brother.

"When you have a problem," said the professor, "you go to its heart. In this case, the heart of the problem is Giant Bat Cave."

"Y-y-you mean we're going into Giant Bat Cave?" said Sister with a shiver.

"Have you ever been in there?" asked Fred nervously.

"Follow me, group," said Actual Factual. He led them out of his office and down a back stair. "Of course I have," said the professor. "Many, many times. It's an important study site. Why, I know Giant Bat Cave as well as I know the palm of my hand." He stopped and looked at the palm of his hand. "As a matter of fact, I may know Giant Bat Cave better than I know the palm of my hand. But, be that as it may, we have places to go and things to do. This way, scouts!"

The back door opened onto the museum's parking lot. Actual Factual's famous sciencemobile was parked there. It was a white van that Actual Factual had fitted out for science work. It had a telescope in

its roof. There were digging tools, ropes, and ladders hooked onto its sides. Inside was a minilab with the chemicals needed to test water and air samples.

The scouts were excited. They had never ridden in the sciencemobile. Now they were going to get their chance. But they were still a little nervous about where they were going. Maybe it was just a "study site" to the professor. But to the members of the Bear Scout troop, Giant Bat Cave was a pretty scary place. It was one they hadn't counted on visiting when they decided to try for the Good Government Merit Badge.

"This isn't the way!" said Fred when Actual Factual turned off the road into the swamp.

"It's a shortcut!" shouted the professor. "But don't worry. I know the swamp well."

The scouts held on tight as the science-mobile rocked and rolled through the muddy swamp.

• Chapter 11 •

HELLO! Hello! Hello!

"Here we are!" shouted the professor. He leaped out of the van and opened the back. He took out a special flashlight. It was hooked to a power pack that Actual Factual slipped onto his back.

The scouts were slow getting out of the van. They stared at the cave's jagged mouth. It looked even scarier in real life than it looked in Ralph's slide.

The professor had gone over to look at a sign that had been put up in front of the cave. "Goodness!" he said. "This is much more serious than I thought." As the scouts joined him, Actual Factual read the sign aloud.

"'Future home of Ralph's Caverama, the Underground Wonderland. Ground-breaking will take place on the twenty-seventh of this month.' And it's signed, 'Ralph Ripoff, President, The Ripoff Company,' and 'Horace J. Honeypot, Mayor.'"

"Good grief!" cried Brother. "That's *tomorrow*!"

"Come!" said Actual Factual. "There's no time to lose. The bats may already have been disturbed."

Actual Factual walked into the cave as if he were walking into his own living room. The scouts followed along behind.

The scouts were nervous. Except for Lizzy, who was more worried about the bats than she was about being scared.

The cave mouth was big enough to drive a truck through. The inside of the cave was even bigger. "Wow!" said Fred. "You could park the Goodbear Blimp in here and it wouldn't even touch the walls!"

Actual Factual turned on the big flashlight. It was very powerful. It cut through the gloom and placed a big circle of light on the roof of the cave. "Good," he said. "The bats look fine. They don't seem to have been disturbed at all."

"Bats?" said Fred, looking up. "I don't see any bats."

The roof of the cave looked like it was lined with black velvet. What the scouts didn't know was that the "black velvet" was thousands of bats hanging upside down.

The professor took some folding field glasses from his pocket. He told the scouts to have a closer look at the roof of the cave. One by one the scouts looked up through the field glasses. They were amazed to see the bats, shoulder to shoulder, sound asleep.

"Aren't they beautiful?" said Lizzy.

"Well," said Sister, "I wouldn't exactly say *that*."

The light was beginning to wake up some of the bats. The professor turned it off. That sent the cave back into a gloomy darkness. But after awhile the Bear Scouts' eyes got used to the darkness and they could see the cave's sharp "teeth."

"Stalactites and stalagmites," said Brother softly.

"Which are which?" asked Sister.

"Here's a little rhyme to help you remember," said the professor.

"Stalactites and stalagmites,
Only caves have got 'em;
'Tites are always up on top,
'Mites are on the bottom."

The professor's rhyme might help them remember which was which. But it also reminded them of Grizzly Grampa's rhyme and got them a little scared again. It was easy to be scared in a place like Giant Bat Cave. It was like a different world. Even the sound was different. Caves are the home of echoes. So the professor wasn't surprised when the scouts started to try some out.

"HELLO!" they shouted, and it came back "Hello! Hello!"

"Please, friends," said Actual Factual. "It's not good manners to come into someone's home shouting at the top of our lungs. Especially the home of bats, who have such good hearing. That's how they catch insects. Flying insects make sound

waves. Bats hear them and catch them in midair."

"I guess that's why, when you see bats just before dark, they fly kind of zigzag?" said Fred.

"Yeah," said Sister, who remembered watching bats at twilight. "Sort of like connect-the-dots. Only the dots are bugs."

"Insects, if you please," said Actual Factual. "But we must not tarry. Come! On with the spelunk!"

"Spelunk?" said Sister.

"*Spelunk*," said Fred. "*To explore caves. Also, spelunking: the sport of exploring caves.*"

The professor had charged ahead into the cave. The scouts had to hurry to catch up.

• Chapter 12 •
A Different World

The professor really did seem to know
Giant Bat Cave like the palm of his hand.
The scouts followed him into a narrow
tunnel. It was getting very dark.

"What's that sound up ahead?" said
Lizzy.

"It sounds like running water," said
Brother.

A fast-running underground river lay
just ahead in the darkness.

"How about your light, Professor?" said
Brother.

"It's much too bright for this part of our
spelunk. Besides, we won't need it. My

new invention, the Handy Dandy
Spelunka-boat, will be much better for
this part of our trip."

That's the way it was with the professor. He always seemed to have a new
invention up his sleeve. Only this one
wasn't up his sleeve. It was in a hiding
place in the cave tunnel. It was hard to
make it out in the dark. But the cubs
would see it soon enough.

The professor pressed a button. There
was a loud hissing sound. Before you could
say Handy Dandy Spelunka-boat, the
scouts were looking at an amazing boat
that glowed like a lightbulb.

"It's nothing, really," said the professor. "I just combined the idea of the self-inflating rubber raft with clear plastic and a gas that glows in the dark."

He pushed the glowing boat into the river and held it while the scouts piled in. He started the motor, and just like that, Professor Actual Factual and the Bear Scouts were putt-putting down the underground river in a boat that glowed like a light bulb. It lit not only the tunnel above but the water below.

"Look!" cried Scout Lizzy. "Fish! Lots and lots of them!"

"I didn't know fish lived in caves," said Scout Sister.

"Of course they do," said Actual Factual as he steered their glowing boat along the winding underground waterway. "All sorts of flora and fauna live in caves."

"Hit it, Fred," said Sister.

"*Flora*," said Fred, "*plants or plant life. Fauna, animals or animal life.*"

The river tunnel had opened up into a great underground room. It had a wide, curved ceiling. There were huge stone pillars made of stalactites and stalagmites that had grown together. It was almost like a palace ballroom. Only instead of a polished floor to dance upon, there was smooth water to float upon.

The only sound was the putt-putt of the motor as the glowing boat steered among the great pillars of stone. The Bear Scouts looked around in wonder as Actual Factual steered for a tunnel at the far end of the room.

"The river tunnel had opened up into a great underground room."

• Chapter 13 •

Daylight Ahead!

"Look!" cried Brother. "Daylight ahead!"

"No," said the professor, with a smile. "It's the light of the most amazing of all forms of cave life: *Lampyrus noctuluca*, better known as 'glowworm.'"

The scouts hardly breathed as they passed through a tunnel lit by the bodies of thousands of glowing worms.

A few more twists and turns, and there really was daylight ahead. It was another cave entrance—a secret one that only Actual Factual knew about. He steered the boat onto a rocky beach that was littered with stalactites that had broken off and fallen. Actual Factual and the scouts pressed the gas out of the boat. Then they rolled it up and put it in another of the professor's hiding places.

The spelunk had been quite an experience. Nobody had spoken for a long time. It was Brother who broke the silence.

"Professor," he said, "there's no question about it. We simply must save this cave. Ralph Ripoff doesn't have to make it into an underground wonderland. It already is an underground wonderland. An absolutely amazing underground wonderland. It must be protected. Will you help us, Professor?"

"With all my heart," said the professor. "What do you want me to do?"

"Come with us to see the mayor. Today! Right now! We're just cubs. But you're a great scientist. Surely he'll listen to you."

"Then let's do it!" cried the professor. He started to leave but stopped to watch the scouts. They had picked up broken

stalactites. They were crossing them like
swords and were about to say their slogan.

The professor picked up a stalactite
and joined them. Their shout of "One for
all, and all for one!" echoed and reechoed
through the cave.

The professor climbed out of the cave
with the Bear Scouts close behind.

• Chapter 14 •

A Meeting with the Mayor

"You may see the mayor now," said the mayor's secretary.

The mayor's office was very important looking. It had important-looking furniture, and there were important-looking paintings on the wall. Mayor Horace J. Honeypot himself was sitting behind an important-looking desk. Standing behind the mayor was Ralph Ripoff.

"Professor Actual! I wid you belcome — er, bid you welcome!" said the mayor with a big smile.

But when Ralph leaned forward and whispered something in the mayor's ear, his smile turned into a frown. "Those bubs—er, cubs—with you," said the mayor, "are the bubs—er, cubs—who made a big fuss at the town meeting!"

"It is because of these bubs—er, cubs—that I am here," said the professor. "Mr. Mayor, you must not go ahead with your plan to destroy that wonder of nature known as Giant Bat Cave!"

"We're not going to destroy it, my fear dellow—er, dear fellow," said the mayor. "We're going to *improve* it."

"That's right," said Ralph. "We're going to turn that worthless hole in the ground into the greatest thing since ice cream cones with jimmies. What's the matter with you, Professor? Are you against progress?"

"I am very much *for* progress, sir," said Actual Factual. "But change is not always progress."

"And what's going to happen to the bats?" said Lizzy.

"And the *Lampy* ... *Lampy* ... the glowworms?" said Sister.

"And the stalactites and stalagmites?" said Fred.

"That's all taken care of," said Ralph. "The mayor has already hired another one of my companies, Ripoff Exterminators, to take care of the bats and all that other cave garbage. We're going to seal the cave off and gas it. Then we're going to bulldoze the whole mess into the swamp."

"Oh, dear! Oh, dear!" said Professor Actual Factual. "You can't do that. It would hurt the ecology of the whole ..."

"Ecology doesn't pay the bills, Professor," said Ralph. He reached over to the mayor's desk and grabbed a fistful of papers. "Contracts, checks, and deals is what pays the bills. Cash, moolah, the long green!"

"Moolah? Long green?" said the professor. "I don't understand."

"It means money, Professor," said Brother.

"Now, if you'll excuse us, Professor," said the mayor, "Mr. Dipoff — er, Ripoff — and I have things to do."

Actual Factual and the scouts turned to leave.

"Just a minute, Professor," said Ralph. "Do you know anything about this?" He took something from his pocket. It was a piece of paper. He unfolded it. He held it up for all to see. This is what it looked like:

Giant Bat Cave
of Beartown Fame
Has the word "giant"
In its name.
Giant Bat Cave...
Think about that.
Which is the giant,
The cave or the bat?
Beware the
VAMPIRE!!!

"The mayor found this nailed to his office door this morning," said Ralph.

"Humph!" said the mayor. "The very idea of a giant bampire vat—er, vampire bat—living in that cave. It's p-p-pure piffle! Sh-sh-sheer cockypop—er, poppycock!"

"And l-l-let me tell you this," said Ralph in an even shakier voice than the mayor's. "If you or anybody else thinks they can scare us off, they've got another think coming! V-v-vampire bat, indeed!"

"What nonsense," said the professor. "Come, scouts. We are wasting our time here."

• Chapter 15 •

The Seed of Fear

The professor and the scouts were looking gloomy as they left the mayor's office. Except for Brother. He had that deep-in-thought look that meant he might be getting an idea.

"Professor," he said, "I don't think we were wasting our time back there. I noticed something that could be important. Ralph and the mayor were a lot more worried about a giant vampire bat than they were about the ecology."

"Brother's right," said Fred. "They were sweating and shaking when they talked about it."

"A giant monster vampire bat," snorted the professor. "Pure piffle. Or as our esteemed mayor said, sheer cockypop — er, poppycock."

They were walking to where the sciencemobile was parked.

"Maybe so, Professor," said Brother, "but look at it this way. You know that vampires are poppycock. And we know that vampires are poppycock. But it looked to me like Ralph and the mayor aren't so sure vampires are poppycock. You saw how they were sweating and shaking about that warning Gramps nailed to the mayor's door."

"Your grandfather did that?" said the professor in a shocked voice.

"Oh, sure," said Brother. "He thinks the only way we're going to save the cave is to beat Ralph at his own game — to trick him, to scare him off. And I think he may be right!"

"What are you saying?" said the professor.

"I'm saying Gramps planted the seed of fear. Now it's up to us to water it and help it grow until ..."

The professor got the message. He finished Brother's sentence. "... until it grows into a giant monster vampire bat that will scare certain bears so bad that they'll never go near Giant Bat Cave as long as they live!"

"Do you think you can do it?" asked Brother.

The professor didn't answer. The Bear Scouts could almost feel Actual Factual's mighty brain powering up for the job of creating a giant monster vampire bat.

"Be at the museum first thing in the morning," said the professor. "Come around to the back door."

The scouts watched as he climbed into the sciencemobile and drove away. They headed home.

• Chapter 16 •

Not a Second to Lose

The Bear Scouts got to the museum bright and early the next morning. But when they went around to the back door, they saw that Grizzly Gramps had gotten there brighter and earlier. At least that looked like Gramps's pickup truck parked beside Actual Factual's sciencemobile.

The scouts went in the back door. Beyond it there was a second door that had a sign on it. The sign said, OPERATION: SAVE THE CAVE — KNOCK BEFORE ENTERING. It was Grizzly Gramps who let them in.

"What are you doing here, Gramps?" asked Brother.

"Shh!" said Gramps. "The professor's been working around the clock and he's hit a rough spot. He called me last night. Said he was going to need my truck for Operation: Save the Cave. So here I am."

The room they were in was Actual Factual's secret workshop. It was the place where he worked on his inventions. There were half-finished inventions around the room. But his latest invention, the one that was supposed to scare Ralph and the mayor out of their wits and save the cave, didn't seem to be going well. There were parts spread all over the floor. Some of the parts looked as if they came from the professor's miniplane.

"What sort of a rough spot?" asked Fred.

The professor was over at the other side of the room, working at his computer.

"It's a little over my head," said Gramps. "As nearly as I can tell, he's havin' trouble findin' the right wing shape for Vee-Bee-One."

"Vee-Bee-One?" said Sister.

"Code name for Vampire Bat One," said Gramps. "I figured a bat wing ought to work. But the professor says no."

Fred looked at the mess of parts spread all over the floor. "Wow," he said. "That looks like something somebody took apart and couldn't put together again."

The scouts went over to where the professor was busily tapping away at his computer. As he tapped, pictures of different kinds of wings showed on the screen. A gull wing, a robin wing, a dragonfly wing. Wing after wing after wing.

"Why not a bat wing?" asked Fred.

"Bats, also birds and insects, fly by flapping their wings. The flapping problem is famous. No inventor has ever solved it. Except for Mother Nature, of course, who is the greatest inventor of them all."

He kept on tapping, calling up one wing after another. Suddenly he leaped up with a startled cry. "Eureka!" he shouted. His chair went over backwards with him in it.

"Fred," said Sister, snapping her fingers.

"*Eureka*," said Fred. "*Cry of joy at the moment of discovery.*"

"Of course!" said the professor as the scouts helped him up. "The pteranodon wing! Pteranodon could flap, but mostly it was a glider. Why didn't I think of it? We have a pteranodon fossil right here in the museum. It's the perfect wing for our purpose!"

The work went quickly after that. As they worked, Actual Factual filled them in on how Vampire Bat One was supposed to work.

"'Supposed' being the key word," admitted the professor. "What I'm doing is combining my miniplane with a helium-filled bat balloon."

"What's helium?" asked Sister.

"It's a gas," said the professor. "The kind they put in birthday balloons that fly away when you let go of the string." The professor went on working as he spoke. "Now, we'll set these little red Christmas tree lights in the head so that the eyes and mouth will glow."

"What are those shells?" asked Lizzy.

"Razor clam shells," said the professor. "They're very light and will make excellent fangs. All right, that does it! We're ready to go!"

"But, Professor," said Brother. "Aren't you going to inflate the bat balloon and put the whole thing together?"

"I wish we could," said the professor. "But it would be much too large to fit in the truck. Somebody would surely see it. Then the bat would be out of the bag. No, we're going to have to load the parts into the truck. Then go through the swamp to the secret cave entrance."

"Why not the main entrance?" asked Brother.

"Because there's a work crew there setting things up for Ralph and the mayor," said the professor. "So we're going to have to use the spelunka-boat to carry everything to the main cave."

"But, Professor," said Lizzy, "that'll take forever!"

"No," said the professor, looking at his watch. "It will take us nine hours and twenty-two minutes, which means we'll have Vee-Bee-One put together in the main cave and ready to fly at sunset. Sunset is very important. First, because that's when Ralph and the mayor are supposed to show up. Two, that's when the thousands of bats will fly out of the cave for their evening meal. And three, because with the sun in their eyes, Ralph and the mayor will be more easily fooled. Now, let's move! There's not a second to lose, and we have a lot of hard work ahead of us!"

• Chapter 17 •

It's a Bird! It's a Plane!
It's a Vampire!

A *lot* of hard work. But by the time the sun had turned red and begun to set, everything was in place.

The scouts were hiding in the bushes at the edge of the swamp. They would be on

the lookout for Ralph and the mayor. When they arrived, Lizzy would signal Actual Factual with a whippoorwill call. Actual Factual would be inside the cave, ready to take off. Gramps was waiting in his truck in a meadow just beyond the swamp.

Then, if all went well, Actual Factual would fly over the swamp and land in the meadow. The scouts would make their way through the swamp over a safe path that Actual Factual had mapped out for them. They would all pitch in and take the vampire apart and load it into the truck. They would zip over to the secret cave entrance and pick up the sciencemobile. Then they would scoot back to the museum before anyone was the wiser.

The mayor and Ralph arrived in the mayor's car just as the sun was setting. They were very pleased with the job that the work crew had done. The sound system was working and the grandstand was ready for the guests who would be arriving later.

"Mr. Mayor," said Ralph, "I think it's safe to say that you and I are about to make a killing. And I don't mean those crummy bats. I mean . . ."

"I know," said the mayor. "You mean mash, goolah—er, cash, moolah, the long green."

Neither Ralph nor the mayor noticed the call of a whippoorwill.

"And speaking of bats," said Ralph, "here come those crummy bats now and . . . AND THEY'VE GOT THEIR BIG BROTHER WITH THEM. THEIR *VERY* BIG BROTHER!"

"It's the vampire!" screamed the mayor. "Run for your life!"

Vampire Bat One flew right at them, its eyes and mouth aglow with red Christmas tree lights. Ralph and the mayor could almost feel the razor-clam-shell fangs on their necks.

"Into the swamp!" screamed Ralph.

Before you could say "oohey, gooey, pewy," Ralph and the mayor were shoulder-deep in the awful swamp mud.

That was the end of Ralph's Caverama.

The invited guests didn't find Mayor Horace J. Honeypot and Ralph Ripoff, President of the Ripoff Company, when they arrived. They found two strange, mud-covered creatures babbling something about ... a giant vampire bat?

It was very embarrassing for the mayor, but not for Ralph. It's not easy to embarrass a crook like Ralph.

• Chapter 18 •

It's Pretty Hard to Impress a Chicken

A few days later the Bear Scouts were relaxing in their secret clubhouse. They were proud of themselves. They had a right to be. They had not only helped save the cave, they had earned not one but three merit badges. That's right, three.

Professor Actual Factual lost no time telling his friend, Scout Leader Jane, the whole story of the saving of Giant Bat Cave. Now the scouts had three new merit badges to add to their honor wall: the Good Government Merit Badge, the Ecology Merit Badge, *and* the Spelunking Merit Badge.

Surely this was a time to say their slogan.
They looked around their clubhouse. There
was nothing to cross.

"Fingers," said Sister.

That's what they did. They crossed fingers
and shouted, "One for all, and all for one!"

Even the chicken who had wandered in was impressed. And everyone knows how hard it is to impress a chicken.

THE Berenstain BEAR SCOUTS
and the
Humongous Pumpkin

THE Berenstain BEAR SCOUTS

and the

Humongous Pumpkin

by Stan and Jan Berenstain
Illustrated by Michael Berenstain

• Table of Contents •

• Chapter 1 •

Now You See Him, Now You Don't

Bear Scouts Brother, Sister, Fred, and Lizzy were having a meeting in their secret clubhouse. No one else knew that the broken-down old chicken coop at the far end of Farmer Ben's farm was really the scouts' clubhouse. Nobody, that is, except Farmer Ben.

It had been a dirty, smelly place when Farmer Ben said they could use it for a clubhouse. But the scouts had worked hard cleaning it and fixing it up. Now it had a table and some chairs. The old

chicken roost was still there. But the
scouts had fixed it up with boards so they
could sit on it. They had made one wall
their "honor wall." The Official Bear Scout
Oath was the most important thing on the
honor wall. It said what the scouts had to
do to be good scouts. It was mostly about
being honest and fair, hardworking and
helpful. This is what it looked like and
this is what it said.

THE BEAR SCOUT OATH

A Bear Scout...

Is as honest as the day is long.
Admits when he or she is wrong.
Respects the creatures of creation.
Views TV in moderation.
Is never cruel, rude, or mean.
Plays the game fair and clean.
Does his or her best at school.
Following the golden rule,
always respects the rights of
    others,
including even sisters' and brothers'.

Signed:
    Scout Brother
    ✿ Scout Sister ✿
    —Scout Fred—
    Scout Lizzy

3

Also hanging on the honor wall were the Bear Scout merit badges the troop had earned. They were pinned to a long ribbon that was tacked to the wall. The scouts had made the old chicken coop into a pretty nice clubhouse — at least from the inside. From the outside it still looked like an old chicken coop. But that was fine with the scouts. It helped keep their clubhouse a secret.

Today's meeting was about trying for another merit badge. "I say we should go for it, said Scout Fred. "You know what they say: 'Nothing ventured, nothing gained.'"

"When they say that," said Scout Sister, "what do they mean?" Sister and Lizzy were younger than Brother and Fred, and Sister thought that Fred sometimes used bigger words than he had to. Lizzy, who was sitting on the chicken roost, didn't seem to be listening. She was looking out the window at some birds in a tree. Suddenly the birds flew away. Somebody had frightened them. That somebody was Ralph Ripoff, Bear Country's leading crook and swindler. What was Ralph Ripoff doing out here in the middle of nowhere?

"Nothing ventured, nothing gained," said Fred, "means that if we don't *try* for the Creative Merit Badge, there's no way we're going to *get* it."

"All right," said Scout Brother. "That's enough arguing. Let's put it to a vote. All those in favor of entering the Spookiest Pumpkin Contest at the Big Pumpkin Festival, say 'aye.' "

Everyone except Lizzy said "aye." Lizzy was still looking out of the window. She had a puzzled look on her face.

"Lizzy," said Brother, "we're taking a vote!"

"About what?" asked Lizzy.

Brother explained about entering the

Spookiest Pumpkin Contest and trying to earn the Creative Merit Badge.

"Oh, sure," said Lizzy. "I vote yes — I mean 'aye.' But gang, something very strange just happened. I mean something *really weird*! You see that tree over there. Well, Ralph Ripoff was standing right beside it and ..."

"What's Ralph Ripoff doing out here in the middle of nowhere?" said Scout Sister.

"... and all of a sudden," continued Lizzy, "*he disappeared!*"

"Disappeared?" said Brother.

"That's right," said Lizzy. "He just plain old-fashioned disappeared!"

"But that's impossible!" said Scout Fred.

"Maybe it's impossible," said Lizzy, "but it happened."

• Chapter 2 •

Bear Country Above,
Weaselworld Below

Many things that seem impossible really are. But others are not.

To see how Ralph was able to disappear right before Lizzy's eyes, let's turn the clock back a couple of minutes to just

before Lizzy saw him through the window.
Before Ralph came into Lizzy's view, he
was walking along, twirling his stick,
singing a song:

Ralph Ripoff
Is my name,
Ripping folks off
Is my game.
I lie, I cheat,
I borrow and beg,
I'm crookeder than
A dog's hind leg.
And what I like
Even better than honey
Is lots and lots
Of other bears' money!

As Ralph walked along, he looked this way and that. He looked at Farmer Ben's old chicken coop. But there didn't seem to be any chickens around. Ralph was on a mission so secret that he didn't even want to be seen by chickens. Even the birds in the tree ahead made him nervous. "Git! Shoo!" he shouted, waving his stick at them. The birds flew away.

Ralph was now standing belly-to-belly with the tree. After one last look around, he reached up and touched a small bump in the tree's bark. At Ralph's touch one side of the tree opened up like a phone booth. Ralph stepped in and the tree closed. Ralph had done exactly what Lizzy said. He had disappeared before her very eyes.

Once inside, Ralph braced himself. This was a trip he had taken many times. But no matter how many times he took it, he was never quite ready for that sudden

start and that awful feeling of falling.

It was even worse than The Space Drop at Grizzlyland, Bear Country's big theme park. Only instead of falling through space in a space car, he was falling through the earth in an earth car. Down through the high-speed tube plunged the earth car. Down, down it fell. It went faster and faster. It was all Ralph could do to keep from screaming. Finally it slowed and came to a stop with Ralph in a lying-down position. The moment it stopped, it popped open and dumped Ralph into a big basket marked "in." Ralph climbed out and dusted himself off. He faced a small, yellow-eyed creature, seated in a great carved chair behind a great carved desk.

"Chief," said Ralph. "We've got to stop meeting like this."

"Welcome to Weaselworld," said Weasel McGreed, head of all the weasels.

• Chapter 3 •

Whatever Happened to "All for One, and One for All"?

"Lizzy, are you sure you saw Ralph standing next to this tree?" said Scout Brother.

The scouts had left their chicken coop clubhouse and come to the place where Lizzy was sure she had seen Ralph disappear.

"Of course, I'm sure," said Lizzy. "He was standing right here, and all of a sudden he was gone."

"Looks like a regular tree to me," said Scout Fred.

"And it feels like a regular tree," said Scout Sister, feeling the bark.

"Hello, there!" called Lizzy. The birds that had flown away were coming back. Most of them lit in the tree's branches. But some of them fluttered down to visit Lizzy. One even lit on her finger. That was the way it was with Scout Lizzy. She had a way with animals — animals of all kinds — from butterflies to bees, from pigs to porcupines. Why, Lizzy could even pet a skunk without getting skunked.

The Bear Scouts were a team and usually got along together very well. But each member of the troop had special abilities. Lizzy had her way with animals. Scout Sister was bold and spunky. Scout Fred was as smart as a whip. He was the sort of cub who read the dictionary and the encyclopedia just for fun. Fred's smarts came in handy sometimes.

Scout Brother was the leader of the

troop. He was its oldest member, but that wasn't the whole reason he was the leader. Mostly it was because he was thoughtful and sensible. Scout Brother was the sort of cub who looked before he leaped and thought before he spoke. He did his share of leaping and speaking, but only after he had done his best to figure things out. That's what he was doing now. Trying to figure out what to make of Ralph's "disappearance."

For starters, he was sure of only two things. First, he was sure that if Lizzy said she saw Ralph disappear, that was what she had seen. Lizzy may have been a bit of a dreamer, but there was no question about her eyesight. She could tell one bird from another a thousand feet away. Lizzy had very good ears, too, though Brother wasn't sure she could hear a mosquito around the corner a block away, as she said she could.

The second thing that Brother was sure
of was that a large bear wearing a plaid
suit and a straw hat and carrying a
walking stick couldn't just "disappear."
There had to be an explanation. But what
was it?

"Lizzy," said Sister. "There's no way you
could have seen Ralph disappear."

"I know what I saw," said Lizzy.

"I say you were daydreaming," said
Sister. "You just *thought* you saw Ralph
disappear."

"I was not daydreaming!" said Lizzy.

"Yes, you were!" said Sister.

"I was not!" shouted Lizzy.

"Were! Were! Were!" shouted Sister.

"Not! Not! Not!" shouted Lizzy.

"Don't you shout at me, Lizzy Bruin!" shouted Sister.

"If you don't get out of my face, I'll do more than shout!" shouted Lizzy.

"Hey, wait a minute," said Scout Fred, stepping between them. "You two are supposed to be best friends."

"That's right," said Brother. "Bear Scouts are supposed to get along with their fellow bears. It says so right in the Bear Scout Oath. And whatever happened to 'All for one, and one for all'?"

That was the Bear Scouts' slogan. They got it from a book that Fred had read. The book was called *The Bear Musketeers*. It was about some soldiers from olden times. They used to cross their swords and shout,

"All for one, and one for all!"

Of course, the Bear Scouts didn't have swords. They looked around for something to cross. All they could find were broken-off branches. The scouts crossed their branches. "All for one, and one for all!" they shouted. The bears' slogan echoed across the rolling hills of Farmer Ben's farm.

ALL FOR ONE, AND ONE FOR ALL!

• Chapter 4 •

Lots to Do

The scouts looked at the tree carefully. They looked all around the tree. But they couldn't find anything the least bit strange.

"Brother," said Scout Fred. "You haven't said what you think about Ralph's disappearance."

"Well," said Brother, "I've been thinking about it. And to tell you the truth, I don't know what to think. . . ." Then, as so often happens when you're trying to figure out something really hard, just when you are about to give up an answer comes to you in a flash.

"The weasels!" said Scout Brother.

"The weasels?" said Scout Fred. "You mean that gang of weasels who are supposed to live underground and are always plotting to steal Bear Country from the bears?"

"That's just stuff that grown-ups tell cubs to scare 'em into being good," said Scout Sister.

"S-s-sure," said Scout Lizzy with a shiver. "Like the bogeybear, and the goblins that'll get you if you don't watch out."

"It was just a thought," said Brother.

But it was more than a thought. Brother had been hearing about the underground weasel gang for a long time. Especially from Grizzly Gramps.

Gramps had a whole scrapbook of bad things that happened. Things that Gramps thought were caused by the weasels. Like when all the honeybees got sick and stopped making honey. Or when the salmon in Great Grizzly River went belly up and died. But nobody took Gramps's ideas seriously. Not even Gran.

"Come on, gang," said Brother. He headed down the road. "We've got lots to do."

"Like what?" said Scout Sister as she and the rest of the troop hurried to catch up.

"First," said Brother, "we've got to stop off at Scout Leader Jane's and get her

okay on trying for the Creative Merit Badge. Then we've got to see about getting some pumpkins to carve for the Spookiest Pumpkin Contest. It's not going to be easy to win that contest. There were some pretty spooky pumpkins last year."

"Y-y-you're telling me," said Scout Sister, with a shiver. Though Sister was bold and spunky about most things, she was a little nervous about spooky things. Sometimes her fellow scouts teased her about it.

"I think we should carve a really scary witch," said Scout Lizzy. She made a scary witch face at Sister and bent her fingers to look like claws.

"I think we should carve a Frankenbear Monster," said Scout Fred. He leaned his head to the side and dragged his foot like the Frankenbear Monster.

"That'll be enough of that!" said Scout Sister.

Now it was Brother's turn. "I think we should carve a vampire," he said, showing his teeth. "Ah, vat a lovely neck you have, my dahling," he said in a vampire accent.

"If you don't cut it out," said Sister, bunching up her fists, "I'll flatten the lot of you!"

The other cubs threw up their hands and backed away in mock fear. But then Sister broke into a giggle. Soon they were all laughing as they walked along.

"After we get our merit badge okay from Scout Leader Jane," said Brother, "I want to stop off at Grizzly Gramps's."

"What for?" asked Scout Lizzy.

"What for?" said Brother. "Guess I can stop off at my own grandfather's if I want to."

• Chapter 5 •

Sealing the Deal

As the Bear Scouts walked along the
sunny Bear Country road, far below a
very strange pair was walking along one
of the spooky tunnels of Weaselworld.
They cast spooky shadows every which
way as they moved along the torchlit
tunnel. There were big broad shadows for
Ralph Ripoff and short skinny shadows
for Weasel McGreed. Armed weasel guards
stood at the ready along the tunnel walls.

"Are you sure you weren't seen?" said
Weasel McGreed.

"I'm sure, chief, I'm sure," said Ralph.

Though it was cool deep underground, Ralph was in a sweat. "There's no way I was seen, chief. This spot is way out in the middle of nowhere. It's way out on the edge of Farmer Ben's farm. The only building around is a broken-down old chicken coop. I mean, there aren't even any chickens around. There's no way I could have been seen. I'd stake my life on it."

"And so you have," said McGreed, his

fierce little yellow eyes gleaming in the torchlight. "This Farmer Ben of whom you speak—does he not grow pumpkins?"

"Oh, sure, chief," said Ralph. By now the sweatband of Ralph's straw hat was soaking wet. He took off his hat and fanned himself with it. "Farmer Ben is a fine pumpkin grower. The best in all Bear Country. Grows beautiful pumpkins. He's won first prize in the Big Pumpkin

Festival six years in a row. Not only are Ben's pumpkins big, round, and orange, they're ..."

"Stop jabbering," snapped McGreed, "and tell me why you have not chosen this Farmer Ben for our little experiment."

"Sure, chief, sure," said Ralph. "Two reasons. First, you said it had to be high ground. It's Papa's pumpkin patch that has the high ground. Overlooks the whole valley. Second, Farmer Ben is a mean, suspicious old cuss. He's the sort who counts his fingers after you shake hands with him. Papa, on the other hand, is a pushover, a natural born sucker. You could steal his underwear before he even felt a draft."

They had come to the place where Ralph had arrived earlier. Next to the big "in" basket, there was a basket marked "out."

"But, chief," said Ralph, "what's this

little experiment all about? Why do you need high ground? And what does it have to do with pumpkins? I mean, I like pumpkins as well as the next fellow. There's pumpkin pie, especially with whipped cream, and pumpkin bread and pumpkin pudding ..."

Weasel McGreed had had enough. "Away with this jabbering fool!" barked McGreed in a low but fierce voice. "Get him out of here!"

The armed weasel guards crowded around Ralph. They started pushing him toward the "out" basket.

"But, chief, haven't you forgotten something?" said Ralph, holding his hand out.

"Pay the jabbering fool," said McGreed.

A henchweasel gave Ralph a bag of money.

"Easy, guys! Easy!" said Ralph. "I'm leaving! I'm leaving! I don't mean to be pushy, chief, but don't you think we ought to seal the deal with a handshake?"

McGreed held his hand out for a brief shake. Ralph climbed into the "out" basket. The moment he settled himself into the earth car, it closed and Ralph was gone.

"I want that fool watched every minute," said McGreed.

"Yes, master," said the head hench-weasel.

Then Weasel McGreed sat in the great carved chair behind the great carved desk. As he did so, the head of all the weasels, ruler of Weaselworld, held up his hand and started counting his fingers.

• Chapter 6 •
Mighty Clever These Weasels

Suppose the Bear Scouts had waited at the trick tree a bit longer. Would the mystery have been solved? The answer is no. That was because one of the trickiest things about the trick tree was its periscope. It was a thing you could look through and make sure nobody was around before you stepped out of the tree.

Mighty clever these weasels, thought Ralph as he checked to see if the coast was clear. Sure that it was safe, Ralph pressed a spot on the wall of the earth car. The tree opened and Ralph stepped out into the bright sunlight.

Too darned clever, thought Ralph as he walked along. Scary little guys. Especially that McGreed. Those nasty little yellow eyes seemed to look right through you. Maybe working for them wasn't such a great idea. If anybody found out about it I'd be in big trouble, thought Ralph. But their money was good. Real good. He squeezed the bag of money in his pocket and felt much better. He did a little jig of joy. Ralph was never so happy as when he was about to trick somebody. Playing old Papa Q. Bear for a sucker would be pure pleasure. But what about the weasels? What were they up to?

Ralph reached into his other pocket. He took out a small envelope. He shook it over his open hand. A single seed fell out. It looked like an ordinary seed. But wait a minute. When Ralph turned his hand a bit, the seed seemed to glow. The glow

worried Ralph. He put the seed back in
the envelope and returned it to his pocket.
What *were* these weasels up to?

The Bear Scouts settled their business
with Scout Leader Jane very quickly. Jane
was always glad to see her troop. But it
was fall break and Jane was busy mark-
ing school papers. Some of those papers

may have been Sister's and Lizzy's. Jane was a teacher at Bear Country School, and Sister and Lizzy were in her class.

"Your Creative Merit Badge plan sounds fine to me," said Jane. She opened the troop record book. "But my records say you still owe me a sleep-out." The troop had been working to earn the Sleep-out Merit Badge. To earn it they would have to have three sleep-outs in one month. So far they had two.

"We're going to be pretty busy, Scout Leader Jane," said Brother, "but we'll do our best to work it in."

With that, the scouts said good-bye to Scout Leader Jane and headed for Gramps and Gran's house.

• Chapter 7 •

More Like a Nightmare

The scouts followed their noses to Gramps and Gran's house. "What's that wonderful smell, Gramps?" called Scout Sister.

Gramps and Gran's house was a great place. It had all sorts of nooks and crannies, porches and towers. The scouts didn't know which was more interesting, the basement or the attic. They were both filled with wonderful old things. The most interesting room in the house was Gramps's den. That's where Gramps worked on his many hobbies. He collected stamps. He made ships-in-a-bottle. He carved amazing little monkey statues out of peach pits.

But let's not forget Gran's kitchen where that delicious smell was coming from.

"As you might expect," said Gramps, "that's the smell of the pumpkin pies Gran's making for the pumpkin festival. This year she's entering four kinds: plain, spicy, with nuts, and with raisins."

"Gran's a sure winner," said Scout Fred, breathing in the great smell.

"Maybe," said Gramps. "But the pie contest is gonna be tough this year. I hear there are some great smells coming out of Widder McGrizz's kitchen, too. And don't forget Mrs. Ben. She's got her pick of Farmer Ben's best pumpkins. By the way, Brother, has your papa given up on the idea of beating Farmer Ben for the biggest pumpkin prize?"

"No, sir," said Brother. "He sure hasn't. He says it's going to be his year to win the big prize."

"That's not gonna be easy," said Gramps. "After all, Farmer Ben is a professional."

"Papa knows that," said Brother. "So he's working extra hard. He's been studying up on pumpkin growing, reading books about it."

"That's right," said Sister. "He's even got this book that says you can make plants grow by talking to them."

"Talking to them?" said Gramps.

"That's right," said Brother. "And it seems to be working. At least he's got some fine-looking pumpkins growing in his patch."

"Well, I guess it can't hurt," said Gramps. "Speakin' of talkin'. Is this a social visit? Or have you cubs got something on your minds?"

"We do have something on our minds, Gramps. It's Ralph Ripoff."

"What's that crook up to now?" said Gramps.

"Disappearing," said Scout Lizzy. "Disappearing is what he's up to."

"Interesting," said Gramps, sitting in his rocker. "Tell me about it."

So Brother, Sister, Fred, and Lizzy all pitched in and told Gramps the story of Ralph's strange disappearance. Gramps rocked slowly as he listened. It wasn't until Brother used the "w" word that Gramps stopped rocking.

"Hmm, disappeared, you say. Right out in the middle of nowhere," said Gramps. "Yes, that *could* have something to do with the weasels."

"I *thought* so," said Scout Brother.

"You mean the weasels are real?" said Scout Fred.

"And not just something grown-ups have dreamed up to scare cubs with?" said Scout Sister.

"More like a nightmare," said Gramps.

• Chapter 8 •

Think Big! Think Round!
Think Orange!

It was true. Papa did have some pretty
fine pumpkins in his patch. And he *was*
talking to them. Papa's pumpkin patch
was on top of a hill. Just beyond Papa's
pumpkin patch was a cliff that looked out
over all of Bear Country. To the right was
the handsome tree house where Scouts
Brother and Sister lived with their mama
and papa. The Bear family's tree house

PAPA'S PERFECT
PUMPKIN PATCH

HAVE A
GOURD DAY!

was almost a home away from home for Scouts Fred and Lizzy. They slept over often.

There was a split-rail fence around Papa's pumpkin patch, and lots of signs. There was a big one that said "Papa's Perfect Pumpkin Patch" and smaller ones that said things like "Have a Gourd Day!" and "Farmer Ben, Say Your Prayers!"

To the left was Farmer Ben's great pumpkin field. Ben had thousands of pumpkins. They looked like great orange jewels resting on their bright green vines.

THINK BIG!
THINK ROUND!
THINK ORANGE!

FARMER BEN, SAY YOUR PRAYERS!

There was a sign on Ben's field, too. It said "Farmer Ben, King of Pumpkins."

We'll just see about that, thought Papa as he urged his pumpkins on. "Grow, my proud beauties! Grow! Suck in that beautiful sunshine! Reach your roots down into that yummy soil and drink up that delicious water, and grow! Think big! Think round! Think orange!"

Papa's pumpkin patch was small. Compared to Farmer Ben's vast pumpkin field, it was tiny. But Papa's patch had some pretty fine pumpkins growing in it — and some big ones, too.

Mama was watching from a tree house window. She was preparing her special pumpkin bread for the festival. Mama didn't think it was Papa's talk that was making his pumpkins grow. She thought it was his hard, careful work. Mama sighed. She did hope Papa would have better luck at this year's pumpkin festival.

• Chapter 9 •

Ralph's Favorite Sucker

"Well, so long, Gramps and Gran!" said Scout Brother.

"And thanks for that yummy pumpkin pie," called Scout Sister.

Gramps and Gran waved from their front porch.

"And thanks for filling us in on those weasels," said Scout Fred. "I think."

"I know what you mean," said Scout Brother.

"Yeah," said Scout Lizzy. "It's pretty scary."

"Well, if any of those weasels ever

bother me," said Scout Sister, "I'll pop him one right on the nose."

"Sure you will," said Brother.

As the troop headed home, the scouts looked nervously at the woods on both sides of the road. If what Gramps had told them was true, the weasels might be watching them at that very moment.

Coming toward the Bear family's tree house from the other direction was none other than the no-longer-disappeared Ralph Ripoff. There was a spring in his step and a twinkle in his eye as he rounded a bend and caught sight of the Bears' tree house. Just beyond it, Ralph could see Papa tending his pumpkin patch. The sight of Papa cheered Ralph so, that he broke into song.

"Ralph Ripoff
Is still my name,
And swindling suckers
Is still my game,
I've got more tricks
Than a dog has fleas,
And now, dear friends,
If you'll excuse me, please,
I see my favorite sucker
Right over there,
Otherwise known
As Papa Q. Bear!"

"Well," said Ralph in a loud jolly voice. "As I live and breathe. It's my great and good friend, Papa Q. Bear!"

"Hi, Ralph," said Papa. "I'm working on my pumpkin patch."

"And what a fine pumpkin patch it is!" said Ralph. "Your pumpkins are a lovely sight to see. And there's no doubt about it, my dear friend, you are sure to win second prize in this year's Biggest Pumpkin Contest at the Bear Country Pumpkin Festival!"

"No, Ralph. You've got it wrong," said Papa. "I'm gonna win *first* prize. I've had enough of second prize. And I've had enough of that show-off Farmer Ben. Calls himself the Pumpkin King. Humph! Well, I'm gonna show him. I'm gonna win *first* prize! Yes sir! *First* prize!

"Now, if you'll excuse me, Ralph. I've got to talk to — er, work on my pumpkins."

Papa began to smooth out the patch with a hoe.

"That's the spirit, Papa Q.!" said Ralph. "Go for it! Look fate in the eye! Dream the impossible dream!"

Papa stopped hoeing. "Impossible?" he said. "You think it's impossible for me to win first prize?"

"Well, of course, nothing's really *impossible*," said Ralph. "I suppose you *could* win first prize. Farmer Ben's pumpkins could be attacked by screw worm and dissolve into orange goo. Or the earth could open up and swallow his whole crop."

"You know those things aren't going to happen, Ralph," said Papa Bear. He sat down on a rock. "Tell me, Ralph. Have you seen the pumpkins Ben's planning to enter?"

"Indeed, I have," said Ralph. "Amazing things. Big as wagon wheels! The color of the setting sun.

"Well, I must be on my way," said Ralph.

Papa sighed a long sigh.

"I guess I'll just have to face it," he said, looking very sad. "There's just no way I'm gonna win first prize."

Ralph had started walking away. But he stopped in his tracks, as if he'd suddenly remembered something very important.

"*Wait a minute!*" said Ralph. He reached into his pocket and took out a small envelope. "*How could I have forgotten?*"

"Forgotten what?" said Papa.

"This!" said Ralph. He looked this way and that, as if he were about to tell a big secret. He shook the envelope over his hand. A single seed fell out.

"A pumpkin seed," said Papa.

"But *what* a pumpkin seed!" said Ralph. "You see, I happen to have a cousin in Big Bear City who is a pumpkinologist."

"A pumpkinologist?" said Papa.

"That's a pumpkin expert," said Ralph. "This, my friend, is a whole new breed of seed."

"It glows," said Papa.

"It glows," said Ralph, "because this little old pumpkin seed is going to grow into ..."

"... a sure-fire guaranteed first-prize winner!" said Papa. "Lemme buy it, Ralph! Lemme! Lemme! Lemme! *Please!*"

Ralph put the glowing seed back into its envelope.

"I'm afraid it's not for sale," said Ralph.

"Not for sale?" said Papa.

"No," said Ralph. "But, my friend, it's yours as a gift." He handed Papa the small envelope.

Papa was speechless. He stared at it as if he had never seen an envelope before.

"G-g-gee, Ralph," said Papa. "I don't know what to say, except thank you, thank you, thank you! I'm gonna plant 'er right now!"

Papa fell to his knees and began digging a small hole.

"Hold on, Papa! Hold on!" said Ralph. "The planting instructions are printed on the envelope."

Papa got up. He began reading the instructions. "'For best results, this seed must be planted at sundown, no later, no earlier. It must be planted three inches deep, no less, no more ...' Hey," said Papa. "This must be some seed."

"And," said Ralph, "it's going to grow into some pumpkin."

"A pumpkinologist, you say," said Papa.

"That's right. Graduated from Pumpkin University. Well, I must be on my way."

Ralph had looked down the road and seen something that made him nervous. Those pesky Bear Scouts were coming.

"Oh, yes, Papa," added Ralph. "That

first-prize pumpkin seed must be our secret. If it gets out that I gave it to you, my cousin could lose his job."

"Mum's the word," said Papa. He put a finger on his closed lips.

"Well, ta-ta," said Ralph. Then he hurried away.

• Chapter 10 •

Follow That Crook

"Hey," said Scout Sister. "Isn't that Ralph talking to Papa right now?"

Even though the scouts were a distance away, they could tell it was Ralph.

"That's Ralph, all right," said Brother. "Come on! We'd better get over there before he sells Papa the sky."

Brother had good reason to worry. Ralph had pulled some pretty raw deals on Papa. There was that honeybee hypnotizer he had sold Papa. It turned out it was just an old eggbeater. Papa had gotten pretty badly stung on that deal. Then there was that driveway topping that never dried. It was like black chewing gum and stuck to everybody's feet.

Ralph was long gone by the time the out-of-breath Bear Scouts reached Papa's pumpkin patch.

"W-what were you and Ralph talking about, Papa?" puffed Scout Brother.

"Nothing special," said Papa. "We were just passing the time of day. He admired my pumpkins, of course, and wished me luck in the Biggest Pumpkin Contest."

"Uh-huh," said Brother.

The scouts looked around. They didn't see any honeybee hypnotizers or cans of black chewing gum. But they were still worried. They moved a distance away and put their heads together.

"I don't like the looks of it," said Scout Brother.

"I think Ralph is pulling some kind of trick on Papa," said Scout Sister.

"I say let's follow him," said Scout Fred. "Maybe he'll give something away."

"Come on!" said Scout Lizzy. "We'll cut across the field. We'll catch up to him and watch him from behind the dry wall."

Within minutes the Bear Scouts were crouching behind the wall that lined the road.

"Here he comes," hissed Scout Sister.

Ralph was quite a sight with his straw hat, flashy suit, and walking stick. His stick flashed in the sunlight as he twirled it. Ralph looked like he didn't have a care in the world as he walked along. And then it happened! The road just seemed to open up and swallow Ralph the way a trout would a fly.

"*Did you see that?*" said Sister.

"I saw it," said Fred. "But I don't believe it!"

"See?" said Lizzy. "That's what happened before. I *told* you I wasn't seeing things!"

"Come on!" said Brother. "Let's check out that spot in the road!"

• Chapter 11 •

"Glumpf! Glumpf!" said Ralph

Far below, deep in the weird underground world of the weasels, Ralph was shooting feet first into the same "in" basket that he had visited earlier. Only this time he was badly shaken. His suit was mussed and he'd lost his hat and stick. As he tried to get up, the stick shot out and poked him, and his hat landed on his head crooked.

"What's going on, chief? Is this any way to treat a trusted employee?" said Ralph.

"Mind your manners, fool," said Weasel McGreed, who was standing by with a

54

gang of armed henchweasels. "I have questions for you, and you had better have the right answers."

"But, chief, look at this suit. I just had it cleaned and pressed," said Ralph as he climbed out of the basket.

"Question one," said McGreed. "Have you carried out my orders to the letter?"

"Absolutely, on the nose, to the letter," said Ralph.

"This Papa Bear has accepted the seed as planned?"

"Yes," said Ralph. "But I gotta ask you, chief. What's this all about? I've got a right to . . ."

"Hush, you fool!" snapped McGreed. "And you're sure he will follow your instructions to the letter?"

"I'm sure," said Ralph. "Old Papa's tongue was hanging so far out for that first prize. . . ."

"Tie him and gag him!" cried McGreed.

Quicker than you can say "welcome to Weaselworld," the weasels had Ralph tied and gagged.

"Glumpf! Glumpf!" said Ralph.

"Trusted employee, indeed!" said McGreed to the struggling Ralph. "You are not worthy of trust. You are a blabbermouth! A loose cannon! A mindless twit! I can't risk your dropping even the smallest hint of our little experiment. So you'll be our 'guest' until it's completed. *Take him away!*"

"Glumpf! Glumpf!" said Ralph as the weasel gang pushed him along the tunnel.

"Speaking of cannons," said McGreed, "are ours in readiness?"

"All is in readiness, master," said the chief henchweasel.

Meanwhile, back up in Bear Country, where the road had swallowed Ralph the way a trout swallows a fly, the Bear Scouts were studying the spot where he had disappeared.

"Look!" cried Scout Sister. "A trapdoor in the road!"

"It says BCEC on it," said Lizzy. "Doesn't that stand for 'Bear Country Electric Company'? I don't get it."

"Maybe you don't get it," said Scout Brother, "but Ralph did."

"You mean . . ." said Sister.

"That's *exactly* what I mean," said Brother, hardly moving his lips. He began walking away. "Come with me. That trapdoor has a lot more to do with the weasel company than with the electric company. And don't look around!"

"Why not?" said Fred.

"Because," said Brother, "we weren't the only ones watching Ralph. The weasels were watching him, too. That's the only way they could have worked that trapdoor at the exact moment he was walking on it."

"I know Ralph is a crook," said Fred. "But I'll never forget his awful scream when he disappeared."

Brother led the troop back over the dry wall and into the field.

"Now here's the deal," said Brother. "Just as sure as one plus one equals two, one disappearing Ralph plus another disappearing Ralph equals . . ."

"Weasels!" agreed the troop.

"Right," said Brother. "So we don't want to fool around with that trapdoor. It could be dangerous."

"This is getting scary," said Scout Lizzy.

"Maybe we should tell our parents, or Scout Leader Jane," said Fred.

"Or the police," said Sister.

"I don't think so," said Brother. "Not just yet. They'll just see where it says Bear Country Electric Company and laugh at us."

"But what are we going to do?" said Fred. "I know Ralph is a crook and all, but . . ."

"We're *doing* it," said Brother. "I think that tree out in the middle of nowhere may be the answer. We'll see if we can figure out how it works. Then we'll go to the police."

The Bear Scouts broke into a run.

• Chapter 12 •

A Tummy-Turning Trip

"It still looks like a regular tree to me," said Fred.

"And it still feels like a regular tree," said Sister.

Lizzy picked up a rock and knocked it against the tree. "Hmm," she said. "It does sound kind of hollow."

The scouts studied every inch of that tree's trunk. But no matter how hard they looked, they couldn't find anything strange.

"Well," said Fred. "We've studied this tree from top to bottom and we haven't found *anything*."

"Just a darn minute," said Sister. "We *haven't* studied this tree from top to bottom. We've just studied the bottom. Gimme a boost."

Scout Brother clasped his hands together and boosted Sister into the tree's branches.

"Hey! Look at this!" said Sister. "The end of this broken-off branch has a glass in it. Like something to look through."

"A periscope!" said Fred.

"Wow!" said Brother. "It's just like Gramps said . . ."

That's when Sister stepped on the bump in the bark and the whole side of the tree opened. The frightened scouts tripped all over themselves and piled up in some weeds. Scout Sister fell out of the tree. But she didn't get hurt, because she fell on her fellow scouts.

"See?" said Lizzy. "I *told* you . . ."

"I know! I know!" said Brother.

The scouts looked inside the tree.

"It's almost like a phone booth with no phone," said Sister.

"Or an elevator with no buttons," said Fred.

Sister, who was always a little too brave for her own good, stepped into the tree.

"Please, Sister!" said Brother.

"Don't be so chicken," said Sister. "Gimme another boost. There's a thing up there to look through."

It took the three of them to boost Sister up. But she never got to look through anything. Because with all four scouts inside, there was enough weight to start the earth car on its tummy-turning downward trip. The tree closed and the scouts were on their way to Weaselworld.

Down, down, down they fell. It was quite an experience. The Bear Scouts screamed all the way down.

After what seemed a long time, but was only seconds, the earth car slowed to a stop. As soon as it stopped, it opened and dumped the scouts into the "in" basket.

• Chapter 13 •

The Rumble of Cannons

The Bear Scouts huddled low in the "in" basket. They were hugging each other and holding hands. They could hear their hearts beating. They hoped no one else would. But there was little danger of that. The tramp, tramp of marching feet and the commands of the weasel captains echoed against the tunnel walls. The Bear Scouts could tell from the sound that the weasel armies were on the march. Huddled in the basket, the scouts remembered what Gramps had said: it was long past time for the weasels to make their move. The tramp, tramp, tramp faded in the distance.

One by one, ever so slowly, the Bear Scouts peeked over the edge of the basket. They could see the last of the weasel army marching out of sight.

"We've got to get away from here!" said Fred in a low voice.

"No," said Brother. "Now that we're here, we have to find out what we can. One thing looks sure. The weasels are going to make a move to take over Bear Country. How did Gramps say it: lock, stock, and honey pot! And we're the only ones who can do anything about it."

"But what can we do?" said Lizzy.

"At least we can look around," said Brother. "Come on."

There were no weasels in sight. The Bear Scouts climbed out of the basket.

"Our best bet is to follow the weasel army," said Brother.

So, staying close to the rough walls, they sneaked along the torchlit tunnel.

"If we're seen, we'll be done for," said Fred.

"That's a chance we'll have to take," said Sister.

The scouts were able to keep hidden in the shadows most of the time. But they were in plain view under the torches. They scurried past those places like bugs caught in the light.

Suddenly a door opened up ahead! Some weasels came out. The Bear Scouts held their breath and hid in the shadows. The weasels were talking in low voices.

The scouts tried to hear what they were saying, but they couldn't. When the weasels moved along the tunnel, the scouts tiptoed to the door. They heard sounds.

"It sounds like lots of hammering and sawing. They must be making something really big," said Sister.

Ever so carefully, the scouts opened the door just a crack. They peeked in. The weasels were making something really big, all right. But there was no telling

what it was. Dozens and dozens of weasels were working on big wooden parts of something.

"What do you think, Fred?" said Scout Brother.

"It looks like parts of a ship, or something," said Scout Fred.

"But that would be like building a ship in your basement, and then you can't get it out," said Scout Sister.

"Somebody's coming!" hissed Scout Lizzy.

The scouts plastered themselves against the wall. The door opened and out came a group of weasel soldiers. One of them wore a cape and a sword and had medals on his chest. He was barking out orders. The others were saying, "Yes, master! Yes, master!" Soon they were out of sight around a bend.

"That must be the guy Gramps told us about. McGreed, king of all the weasels," said Brother.

"I say let's go back to that earth car," said Fred. "What comes down must go up. Let's go back to Bear Country and warn somebody!"

"Warn them about what?" said Brother. "Warn them that there's a weird bunch of weasels marching back and forth who are building something. But we don't know what. No, we need to find out more. We need to find out exactly how they're planning to take over Bear Country."

The scouts moved on. There was another, much larger door up ahead. It was the kind that opens up like a garage door. There was a smaller door beside it. The scouts opened it a crack and peeked in. There were no weasels inside. But there was a weird-looking machine. It was huge! It had great wheels with studded truck tires and a tank as big as a small house. But the strangest thing about it was the part that pointed up in the air. It looked almost like a giant Dustbuster reaching for the ceiling.

The scouts heard a loud rumbling noise in the tunnel behind them. They slipped into the room with the strange machine and watched. This time there was no question about what they were looking at. They were looking at *cannons*. Lots and lots of cannons being pulled along by

teams of weasels. Behind the cannons were wagons piled high with cannonballs.

"*Now* can we go back to Bear Country and tell them what we saw?" said Scout Fred.

"I still wish we knew *how* the weasels are going to attack Bear Country," said Brother. "But you're right. It's time to go back. . . . But wait! What's that over there?"

Sister reached down and picked it up. "It's Ralph's walking stick!" she said. "I'd know it anywhere. And look there! If that isn't Ralph's straw hat, I'll eat it!"

The hat was kind of battered. It was on the floor beside a closet door. A muffled "Glumpf! Glumpf!" came from inside the closet. Brother opened the door. There was Ralph all trussed up like a Christmas turkey.

"Glumpf! Glumpf!" said Ralph.

• Chapter 14 •

Lucky for Ralph, Bear Scouts Are Good at Knots

First, the scouts removed Ralph's gag. "You crazy cubs!" he cried. "What are you doing here? If the weasels find you, you're done for!"

The scouts went to work on the knots that held Ralph tight.

"Never mind about that, Ralph," said Scout Brother. "What's going on down here? And what do you have to do with it?"

"Who, me?" said Ralph. "I don't have *anything* to do with it. I was walking along as nice as you please and *whammo*,

I'm down here tied up tighter than a tick ... ! Oh, look what they did to my hat! Oh, dear!"

"Never mind about your hat!" said Brother. "What was going on between you and Papa today?"

"Nothing! Nothing at all!" said Ralph. "I swear on my sainted mother's lace shawl! It was about a pumpkin seed, that's all. The weasels paid me a modest sum to get Papa to plant a pumpkin seed. What possible harm could there be in a little pumpkin seed?"

"I don't know about pumpkin seeds," said Brother. "But there could be lots of harm in cannons."

"Lots of 'em!" said Sister.

"And cannonballs!" said Lizzy.

"And some kind of war machine!" said Fred. "And maybe even a warship!"

"Cannons?" said Ralph. "And cannonballs? And war machines? Goodness gracious me! This *is* serious! I don't know anything about that. But I do know we've got to get out of here and back to Bear Country. Look, you all sneak back to the earth car. Just get into it and it'll take you back up. It's automatic."

"What about you?" said Lizzy.

"Don't worry about me," said Ralph. "I know twenty-seven ways of getting out of here. But there's one very important thing. You must never tell anyone about me and the weasels. If you tell, the bears will tar and feather me and ride me out of town on a rail—a splintery rail! Now, get back to that earth car!"

• Chapter 15 •

The Good News and the Bad News

With all the weasels moving in the other direction, the scouts got back to the earth car with no trouble. Ralph was right. It worked automatically.

The scouts were back up in Bear Country, safe and sound. But what to do? The scouts talked about it as they hurried back to the tree house and Papa's pumpkin patch.

"What do you think we ought to do?" said Scout Fred.

"It's hard to say," said Brother. "What

we have is a good news, bad news situation. The good news is that we found out that the weasels are gonna make some big move; the bad news is that we can't tell anybody about it."

"Why not?" said Sister.

"Because," said Scout Brother, "nobody will believe us. They'll say we're just a bunch of silly cubs making up stories. And I wouldn't blame them."

"But Ralph will back us up," said Scout Fred.

"No, he won't," said Brother. "He'll lie through his teeth. And I wouldn't blame *him*, either. You heard what he said. If the bears found out he was working for the weasels, they'd ride him out of town on a splintery rail. And I wouldn't blame *them*. No, we've got to cool it. We've got to keep our eyes and ears open and be ready for anything.

"What puzzles me," Brother went on, "is

what do cannons and soldiers have to do with a pumpkin seed and Papa's pumpkin patch?"

"Maybe," said Scout Fred, "that pumpkin seed is really a tiny radio sending out signals."

"A radio in a pumpkin seed?" said Scout Sister.

"It's possible," said Fred. "Scientists can do all kinds of stuff like that. I've heard they can fit a minicam into a green pea. And there's a video game coming out that you can wear in a ring."

"What kind of signals?" said Brother. Scout Fred shrugged.

"Hey, maybe we should tell Gramps," said Scout Sister. "He'd believe us."

"Yeah," said Brother. "But nobody will believe Gramps. Like in that old story, 'The Bear Who Cried Weasel.' "

As the Bear Scouts rounded a bend in the road, the Bear family's tree house came into view. There was Mama putting in some fall plants. On the high ground, there was Papa tending his pumpkin patch as calm as you please.

"You know what?" said Scout Sister. "I'm hungry."

"Hungry as a bear?" said Lizzy.

"You got that right!" said Sister. Mama always had cold milk and sandwich makings, and maybe even some fresh-baked cookies. The scouts put on speed and headed for Mama's kitchen.

• Chapter 16 •

The Humongous Pumpkin

After a meal of sandwiches and milk and cookies, the Bear Scout troop worked out a plan. They would act like nothing special was about to happen. The fact was, they couldn't figure out how anything *was* about to happen. At least not any time soon.

It was one thing for the weasels to play soldier down there in Weaselworld. But up here in Bear Country they wouldn't have a chance, cannons or no cannons. They would be up against *bears*. Why, powerful Papa could flatten the lot of them all by himself.

But, as Gramps said, the weasels were smart. So it was a good idea to stay on the lookout for signs of trouble. A key part of the scouts' plan was to keep a watch on Papa's pumpkin patch. That's where they would do the sleep-out they owed Scout Leader Jane.

Meanwhile, they got some small pumpkins from Papa and began getting ready for the Spookiest Pumpkin Contest. They set up in Papa's workshop. Lizzy was a very good artist. She made a witch sketch, a Frankenbear sketch, and a vampire sketch.

"Ooh!" said Scout Sister when she saw the sketches. Her fellow scouts thought it was pretty funny how brave Sister was about real things and how scared she was of things that weren't real.

When Lizzy finished her sketches, the scouts went to work carving the spooky pumpkins — except for Sister. She took the job of cleaning out the pumpkins' insides. She borrowed Mama's big ice cream scoop and went to work. Pretty soon she had a bucket overflowing with pumpkins' insides. It was a wet, gloppy, seedy mess.

The pumpkins were about half carved and looking pretty spooky when it began to get dark. The scouts set up their sleep-out camp right next to Papa's pumpkin patch. The troop had a delicious sleep-out supper. There's nothing yummier than hot dogs roasted on green sticks over a campfire and topped off with hot cocoa. Then they slipped into their sleeping bags and tried to go to sleep. It wasn't easy with all that was on their minds. But they'd had a long, hard day — and after a while they fell asleep.

Pretty soon Sister began to have a dream. But let's not mince words. Sister began to have a galloping rip-roaring nightmare! It wasn't the spooky pumpkins she dreamed about, the witch, the monster, or the vampire. It was the pumpkins' insides she dreamed about — those wet, gloppy, seedy insides. In the dream they rose up out of the bucket and formed into a wet gloppy weasel. A *giant* wet gloppy weasel. As soon as it formed, it began to

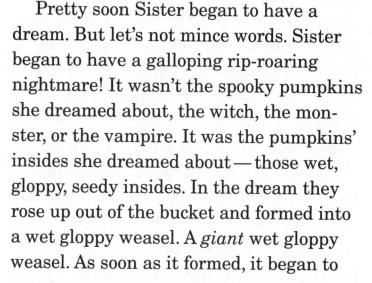

chase Sister. She ran as fast as her legs could carry her. But the weasel monster kept getting closer and closer. The monster was just about to get her when she tripped over some kind of giant root and woke up.

But it turned out not only that the giant root was real, it was a giant *pumpkin* root. It had grown under her sleeping bag and lifted her up in the air. And it was still growing! That wasn't all that was still growing. Sister couldn't believe her eyes when she saw it. It was a humongous pumpkin. It was already as big as a house and it was still growing.

I must still be dreaming, thought Sister, but *maybe not!*

There was only one way to find out. Sister pinched herself *hard*. *"Ouch!"* she hollered.

Sister's "ouch" woke the others. Sister pointed at the humongous pumpkin. "I thought I was dreaming," she cried.

"It's no dream," said Brother.

"It's a living weasel nightmare!"

"You're right!" said Scout Fred. "It all makes sense now. The seed, the soldiers. That machine is a sucking machine. For sure, it's already sucking that pumpkin's insides into that giant tank!"

Lizzy had climbed up onto a giant pumpkin vine and was putting her extra-special good hearing to work. She put her ear to the pumpkin. "It's the weasels, all right. I can hear that one with the cape, the sword, and the medals, giving orders."

"That's McGreed!" said Brother.

"Look!" cried Scout Fred. Rows of square openings were being cut from the inside. "They're *gunports*!"

And, sure enough, cannons were poking out of the openings as soon as they were cut.

"That wasn't a warship they were working on," cried Fred. "It was a *war pumpkin*!"

The Bear Scouts knew that if they didn't do something all would be lost. And they had to do it *now*! With the weasels in control of the high ground, all of Bear Country would be under the weasel guns.

"We've got to do something!" cried Brother.

"But what?" cried Sister.

"What *can* we do?" cried Lizzy.

"Excuse me, friends," said Scout Fred. "But there was an ancient wise bear who said . . ."

"Please, Fred," said Brother. "This isn't the time for ancient wise bears. The weasels are about to take over Bear Country!"

"Lock, stock, and honey pot!" wailed Sister.

"Oh, dear! Oh, dear! Oh, dear!" cried Lizzy.

"I repeat," said Fred. "There was an ancient wise bear who said . . ."

"Fred, you shut up about ancient wise bears," cried Brother.

Scout Fred decided it was time to "show" rather than "tell." He picked up a long fence rail. ". . . an ancient wise bear who said, 'Give me a lever and a place to stand and I can move the world!'" He put one end of the fence rail under the pumpkin. Then he rested the rail on a rock and began pulling down on the long end. The humongous pumpkin began to tip just a little.

"How about four levers!" cried Brother.

Within seconds there were four fence-rail levers in place and four Bear Scouts pulling down on them.

"Heave ho! Heave ho!" shouted the scouts. The pumpkin was now tipping quite a lot.

Meanwhile, up in the tree house, the shouts of the scouts woke Papa. He went to the window to see what the noise was

about and saw the biggest pumpkin the
world had ever seen. The sight thrilled
Papa down to his very toes.

It was the last "heave ho!" that did it.
The humongous pumpkin tore loose —
vine, roots, weasels, and all. It rolled to the
edge of the cliff and crashed down into the
valley with the biggest SPLOOSH ever
heard in Bear Country.

It was still too dark to see what sort
of mess it made or what happened to the
weasels and their cannons. But the scouts
really didn't care what happened to the
weasels. What they cared about and were

proud of was that they had saved Bear
Country!

The Bear Scouts looked at each other.
They knew that this was a special
moment. It was time to say their slogan.

The fence rails were big and heavy, and it wasn't easy to cross them. But they managed to do it.

"All for one, and one for all!" they shouted.

Papa had thrown on his clothes and gotten outside just in time to see the humongous pumpkin roll off the cliff and crash into the valley. Papa rushed over to the great torn place where the pumpkin had grown.

"My pumpkin!" he cried. "My surefire, couldn't-miss, guaranteed first-prize-winning pumpkin! What happened to it?"

"Well, Papa," said Sister, taking him by the hand. "It just sort of tipped over."

"There'll be other pumpkins, Papa," said Brother.

"But not like that one," said Papa. "That pumpkin was ... *humongous*!"

"Papa," said Brother. "You've sure got that right."

ALL FOR ONE, AND ONE FOR ALL!

• Chapter 17 •

The Best Good Deed

Papa came in his usual second to Farmer Ben in the Biggest Pumpkin Contest. The Bear Scouts came in only third in the Spookiest Pumpkin Contest. But that was good enough to earn the Creative Merit Badge. They also earned the Sleep-out Merit Badge, of course.

But the Bear Scouts not only did not earn a merit badge for saving Bear Country from the weasels, they couldn't even tell anybody about it. They wanted to, but Gramps convinced them that nobody would believe them. He convinced

them of that by taking them to all the
places where the weasels might have left
a trace. He opened the electric company
trapdoor. All that was down there was
wires. As for that tree in the middle of
nowhere — it was gone! They even checked
out the valley into which the humongous
pumpkin had splooshed. They couldn't
find a trace.

"I told you," said Gramps. "That's the
way it is with the weasels. They never
leave a trace."

"Gee," said Scout Sister. "We did this
great thing and nobody knows about it."

"*You* know about it," said Gramps. "And
here's a little rhyme I'd like you to think
about:

"There are good deeds large
And good deeds small,
But the good deeds which
Are best of all
Are those unknown
Except to us,
That win us no
Applause or fuss,
The deeds we feel
Deep inside,
In which we take
The greatest pride."

The scouts looked out over beautiful, bountiful Bear Country.

"I'll buy that," said Scout Brother.

"Me, too," said Scout Sister.

"Me, too," said Scout Fred.

"And so will I," said Scout Lizzy.

Then they headed for Gramps and Gran's for some of Gran's first-prize-winning pumpkin pie. It was delicious!

THE *Berenstain* BEAR SCOUTS
Meet
BIGPAW

THE Berenstain BEAR SCOUTS
Meet
BIGPAW

by Stan & Jan Berenstain
Illustrated by Michael Berenstain

• Table of Contents •

• Chapter 1•

Exciting Plans

It had been a disappointing winter for the Bear Scouts. Oh, they'd had fun. They had gone sledding on Dead Bear's Hill, ice fishing on Lake Grizzly, and skating on Farmer Ben's duck pond. But they hadn't been able to do much scouting. They did earn one merit badge. It was for cross-country skiing. That was because the snow was so deep, skis were the only way they could get to school during much of the winter.

But now the sun was riding higher in the sky and the first signs of spring were

beginning to show. There was still lots of
snow. But here and there, blue and yellow
crocuses were starting to peep through. As
juncos and other snowbirds headed north,
their places were being taken by robins
and mockingbirds.

There was still enough snow on the
ground so that Scouts Brother, Sister,
Fred, and Lizzy were able to cross-country
ski all the way to their secret chicken-coop
clubhouse at the far edge of Farmer Ben's

farm. There wasn't any heat in their clubhouse. So it was almost as cold inside as it was outside. The bundled-up scouts gathered around Scout Brother, who was looking through *The Bear Scout Handbook.* Now that spring was on the way, the Bear Scouts were looking for something exciting to do.

"Here it is," said Scout Brother. "Merit badges."

"Yeah," said Scout Fred. "Let's find an exciting one to try for."

"Hmm," said Scout Brother. "How about Computer Merit Badge?"

"Don't think so," said Scout Lizzy.

"Mapmaking Merit Badge?" said Scout Brother.

"Not exactly exciting," said Fred.

"Basket-weaving Merit Badge?" said Brother.

"Forget it!" said Sister.

"Hey, here's one that sounds exciting," said Brother. "Rock-climbing Merit Badge!"

"Now you're talking!" said Lizzy.

"That's more like it!" said Fred.

"I can see us now," said Sister. "All harnessed together as we rock-climb up the sheer face of some mighty mountain."

"Wait a minute," said Scout Lizzy. "What's that little mark after where it says 'Rock-climbing Merit Badge'?"

"That's an asterisk," said Fred.

"An aster—what?" said Sister.

"*Asterisk*," said Fred, who read the dictionary just for fun, "pronounced *AS-ter-isk: the mark used in printing to indicate a footnote.*"

"All right, Mr. Smarthead. I'll bite," said Sister. "What's a footnote?"

Fred pointed to the bottom of the page. There was another asterisk with some words beside it. "That," he said, "is a footnote."

Brother read the footnote aloud. " 'Bear Scouts earning this badge must be supervised by a qualified adult.' "

The Bear Scouts' smiles turned into frowns.

"So much for rock climbing," said Scout Lizzy.

"I can see us now," said Scout Sister. "Up to our ears in reeds and straw, trying for that good old Basket-weaving Merit Badge."

"Don't give up on rock climbing so fast,"

said Scout Brother. "Don't we know a qualified adult who might be willing to help us? Think about it."

The rest of the troop thought about it.

"Of course!" they shouted. "Professor Actual Factual!"

"Right!" said Scout Brother. "He's always climbing up some cliff to collect plants and moss and stuff. I'll bet he's climbed just about every rock, cliff, and mountain in Bear Country!"

Things were looking up. Professor Actual Factual was a good friend and was usually willing to help.

"Slogan time!" said Scout Brother.

He picked up a ski pole. The other scouts did the same. Then, with their ski poles crossed, they shouted, "One for all! And all for one!"

"Do you really think Professor Actual Factual will agree to help us get our Rock-climbing Merit Badge?" said Scout Fred.

"There's only one way to find out," said Brother. "Let's go ask him."

Pretty soon the Bear Scouts were skiing toward the Bearsonian Institution, which was the home and workplace of Professor Actual Factual, Bear Country's leading scientist. It was a little tricky because the snow was getting patchy. In a couple of places they had to take the long way around.

ONE FOR ALL!
AND ALL FOR ONE!

• Chapter 2 •

Something's Coming!
Something Big!

Far to the south, in a strange and distant place called Sinister Swamp, there wasn't a trace of snow—or even much dry land. There were just trees and muddy water as far as the eye could see. Which wasn't very far, so thick were the tangled vines and mosses that hung from the trees.

All was quiet in Sinister Swamp except for the drip drip drip of the wet vines, the sound of a frog plopping into the muddy water, and the splash of a fish reaching for a low-flying dragonfly. All was still, except for a lizard who was tasting the air, a snapping turtle who was looking for lunch, and a great horned owl who glided down for a snack of snake.

But wait. Something was happening in Sinister Swamp. Something strange. Something frightening. Frogs, lizards, and snapping turtles made themselves scarce. Great Horned Owl hid under its own wing. Even the huge swamp crocs, who feared nothing, hunkered down and pretended they were half-sunken rotting logs. It was as though some swamp radar had warned the creatures of Sinister Swamp that something was coming. Something big!

• Chapter 3 •

The Professor Works Things Out

"As I understand it," said Professor
Actual Factual, "you want me to help
you earn the Rock-climbing Merit
Badge."

"That's right, professor," said Scout
Brother.

"Be happy to do so," said the professor.
"As a matter of fact, I'm planning some
fossil hunting in the mountains. So your
timing is excellent.

"Now, if you'll excuse me, friends, I
must be getting back to my office. I have a
great deal to do! . . . "

"But, professor," said Scout Sister. "You *are* in your office."

The professor looked around. "So I am! So I am!" he said. "My goodness! It *is* a mess, isn't it? Well, you just bring me a note from Scout Leader Jane—and how *is* that dear sweet person?—and we can begin fitting you out for rock-climbing gear."

"Er—that's another thing, professor," said Brother. "Scout Leader Jane might be a little nervous about our going for the rock-climbing badge. It might help if you talk to her about it."

"Fine," said the professor, reaching for the phone. "I'll call her right now."

"Why don't you wait till the party?" said Brother. "You'll both be there."

"Party?" said the professor. "What party?"

"This one," said Scout Lizzy, who had fished an invitation out of the jumble of mail on Actual Factual's desk.

"Ah, yes!" said Professor Actual Factual. "Readings by Grizzly Gran. Nonsense, of course. But charming nonsense."

It was settled. The professor would work things out with Scout Leader Jane. The Bear Scouts said good-bye, got back on their skis, and headed home.

It's A Party!

Readings by Grizzly Gran
Time: 2:00 P.M.
Place: The Tree House

• Chapter 4 •

Much, *Much* Bigger Than the Average Bear

Meanwhile, back in Sinister Swamp, fear was in the air. Something was coming! Something big! But what was it?

Whatever it was, the thunder of its mighty footsteps could be heard in the distance—and felt. The whole swamp seemed to shake as it pounded closer and closer.

To the pounding footsteps, add the crackle and crash of undergrowth and thicket, even trees, being torn away. When at last it broke through the tangled tick-tacktoe of tree and branch, the swamp creatures couldn't believe what they saw. It was a bear. But what a bear! A *monster* of a bear! Much, much, *much* bigger than the average bear. With legs like trees with knees. Feet like hay bales. Shoulders like boulders. And arms that just didn't quit. And at the ends of those arms: *BIG PAWS!* One of those paws tore at the tangle. The other held a club the size of a small tree. *Correction.* It wasn't a club at all, but some sort of great log banjo.

As the gigantic banjo-carrying bear moved through the forest, he began to sing. As he sang, he strummed. And so, strumming and singing, he told one and all who he was and what he was about.

YOU CAN HAVE YOUR
SASQUATCH,*
YOUR A-BOM-IN-A-BLE SNOW-
MAN,*
MY NAME IS BIGPAW,
I'M BIGGER THAN 'EM ALL!

ONE THING I LIKE TO DO IS EAT.
AND WHEN I EAT,
I CHOMP AND CHAW,
AND GRIND AND TEAR,
AND RIP AND CLAW!

SO REMEMBER MY NAME,
MY NAME IS BIGPAW!

* Sasquatch: hairy creature said to live
in the Olympia mountains of the United
States Northwest.

*Abominable snowman: hairy creature
said to live in the Himalayan mountains
of central Asia.

The swamp creatures watched him tear off a tree branch and chew it up as if it were a stalk of celery. He was something to see, this giant bear who shook the very air with his strumming and singing. Frogs, lizards, and turtles watched from their hiding places. Great Horned Owl cracked an eye and stared. Even half-sunken rotting logs opened their yellow eyes and took in the show.

YOU CAN HAVE YOUR SASQUATCH,
YOUR A-BOM-IN-A-BLE SNOWMAN,
MY NAME IS BIGPAW,
I'M BIGGER THAN 'EM ALL!

SOMETHING ELSE I DO IS DANCE,
AND WHEN I DO,
I WHOMP AND TROMP,
I POUND THE GROUND,
AND SHAKE THE SWAMP!

SO REMEMBER MY NAME,
MY NAME IS BIGPAW!

As good as his word, the great creature
not only shook the swamp, he left all the
swamp creatures badly shaken. They'd remember his name, all right. As the giant
bear crashed out of sight, they all
breathed a sigh of relief.

• Chapter 5 •

Grizzly Gran Does Her Thing

The Bear family and their neighbors welcomed spring each year with a street party. The road between the Bear family's tree house and Farmer Ben's farm was closed to traffic. Banners were stretched across the road, and party balloons were tied to fence posts. It was a covered-dish party. All kinds of Bear Country goodies were brought by the guests. It was a friendly party, with folks getting back in touch after a long hard winter. Farmer and Mrs. Ben were chatting with Mama and Papa Bear. Even Chief Bruno and Ralph Ripoff, who didn't always get along, seemed to be getting along.

"What's *he* doing here?" said Farmer Ben.

"I'm afraid Papa invited him," said Mama.

"Ralph's not so bad," said Papa. "He's got some good ideas."

"The trouble," said Mama, "is that most of them are crooked."

"Well, I just don't trust anybody who wears a straw hat and spats," grumped Farmer Ben.

The Bear Scouts had had their share of run-ins with Ralph. But at the moment, they were much more interested in the talk that was taking place between Scout Leader Jane and Professor Actual Factual.

"Do you think Scout Leader Jane will go along with our rock-climbing idea?" said Scout Lizzy.

"My guess is yes," said Scout Fred. "The professor can wrap Scout Leader Jane around his little finger."

"I don't know about little fingers," said Scout Brother. "But the professor is giving us a 'thumbs-up.' "

"Way to go!" said Scout Fred.

"Great Grizzly Mountains, here we come!" said Scout Sister.

The Bear Scouts were feeling good. They were on their way to a really big-time merit badge. It felt like slogan time. But the scouts never did their "all for one" slogan in public. So they quietly exchanged low fives. Then they joined the rest of the guests. Papa was about to make an announcement. He climbed up on a stump and called out over the party chatter,

"Come close, friends,
and welcome spring!
Watch Grizzly Gran
do her thing!"

Grizzly Gran's "thing" was fortune-telling. Gramps liked to tease her about it. "Yep," he liked to say, "Gran'll read anything: crystal balls, palms, tea leaves, left-over mashed potatoes, dust devils under the bed—anything!" Which wasn't exactly true, but almost. Her favorite thing to read was a dripping, honey-rich honeycomb. And her favorite time to read it was the spring party.

The guests gathered round. They looked forward to Gran's readings. They knew it was all in fun. But sometimes she got things right. Like the time she predicted that Bess, Mizz McGrizz's old hound dog, would have septuplets. "If you predict enough stuff," pooh-poohed Gramps, "you're *bound* to get something right." Maybe so. But there was an air of excitement as everybody, including the Bear Scouts, gathered close.

Everything was ready. Papa had Mama's big black frying pan. Mama held a bag of flour. Papa placed the frying pan on the stump. Mama sprinkled flour into the pan until its bottom was white. Gramps tied a piece of string to the honeycomb.

It may have been all in fun, but even Professor Actual Factual watched closely as Gran held the dripping, dribbling honeycomb over the frying pan. Ever so gently, she let it swing to and fro, round and round over the flour-coated pan. As she did so, she said in her spookiest fortune-telling voice:

"Honeycomb dribble,
Honeycomb drip,
What holds the future?
Big money?
A trip?

Grizzly black,
Grizzly gray,
Tell us the future.
Tell us today!"

Then *poof!* Gran blew as hard as she could. The flour that wasn't stuck to the pan made a great cloud. Since Gramps was closest, most of the flour got on him. The Bear Scouts laughed. "You look like a ghost, Gramps," said Scout Sister.

But it was Gran, staring at the flour left in the pan, who looked like she had *really* seen a ghost. Because there in the frying pan was a giant flour footprint.

Gran stared at it as if it were the last thing she wanted to see. "The sign of Bigpaw!" she gasped. Then she added, in a frightened whisper, *"And he's headed this way!"*

"Oh, dear!" said Mama.

"Impossible!" said Papa.

"Gracious!" said Mrs. Ben.

"If he shows up at my place, I'll be ready with a loaded shotgun," said Ben.

"Now, Ben," said Chief Bruno. "I'll have no taking the law into your own hands."

"I must gaution you, Cran—er, caution you, Gran," said the mayor, who had a way of getting the fronts and the backs of his words mixed up, "a prediction like that could pause a canic—er, cause a panic!"

"Can't help that, Mr. Mayor!" said Gran. "Goodness! Don't you think I'd rather predict septuplets or a good corn crop if it was up to me? But it's not up to me. I gotta call 'em as I see 'em. Predictin'

gives me a appetite. Come on, Gramps.
Let's put on the feed bag."

The crowd began to drift toward the
food table. The Bear Scouts found themselves next to the professor. "It's all set,"
he said. "Be at the Bearsonian tomorrow
morning for your first rock-climbing lesson."

"We'll be there," said Scout Brother.
"And thanks for working things out with
Scout Leader Jane. But I have a question,
professor: *What the heck is Bigpaw?*"

The professor chuckled. "No disrespect
to your grandmother, of course. But it's
pure superstition. There is not, never was,
and never will be any such thing as Bigpaw. On second thought, let me change
that: Take out 'never was.' But come! Let
us put on the feed bag—er, let us seek
refreshments."

• Chapter 6 •

A Cave with a View

Mountain goats were very much at home on the rocky ledges of Table Rock Mountain. The tough, sure-footed mountain goats made out fine on its high, narrow ledges. The mountain gave them everything they could want: grass and moss when they were hungry, ice and snow when they were thirsty, and a view money couldn't buy.

And early one spring afternoon, it gave them the shock of their lives. When the sure-footed mountain goats saw Bigpaw, they almost lost their footing. Goat

mouths fell open. Goat eyes opened wide.
Goat beards trembled.

Up the mountain he came, and up the
mountain he went. The great monster of a
bear climbed the mountain as easily as a
cub climbs a jungle gym. Up, up he went
with his log banjo slung over his shoulder.
He climbed until he came to a broad ledge,
just under Table Rock.

A cave opened onto the ledge. Bigpaw
looked into the cave. He had come a long
way. He was very tired. He unslung his
banjo. He stood on the ledge and looked
out over the valley. It was very beautiful
in the afternoon sun. Bigpaw stretched. As
he stretched, he yawned. Just as Bigpaw
was mighty, so were his yawns. They
echoed through the valley like thunder.
Then Bigpaw entered the cave and went
to sleep.

• Chapter 7 •

Tell Us More About This Bigpaw, Professor

The rumble of Bigpaw's yawns echoed across the valley. It reached the Bear family's street party. It was refreshment time. Farmer Ben was in the food line with Actual Factual and the Bear Scouts. Ben looked up. "Not a cloud in the sky and we're getting thunder," he said. "But it's kinda early for a thunderstorm. Wouldn't you say so, professor?"

"I'd say so, Ben," said the professor. Actual Factual knew better than to discuss weather with him. Being a farmer,

Ben had strong opinions about it.

"You'd think Gran would have predicted something useful. Like the weather," said Ben. "Instead of that foolishness about Bigpaw. Why, that story's been kickin' around for years and he ain't never showed up yet. I'll take my pitchfork to him if he ever shows up around my place."

The line had moved, and it was Farmer Ben's turn at the food table. He loaded his plate with goodies. When Actual Factual and the scouts reached the food table, they did the same. They saw a good place to sit across the yard. It was a special bench that Papa had built around a big oak tree.

"Professor," said Scout Brother when they were settled. "Would you tell us more about this Bigpaw?"

"There's nothing to tell," said the professor. "Bigpaw is a myth, he doesn't exist. Let me explain." The professor took a pickle from his plate. "See this pickle? It exists. It's real." He smelled the pickle. "It has a smell." He took a bite of the pickle. "It has a taste . . . um, it's delicious! Crunchy!" He took another bite, and another and another, until the pickle was gone. "So you see," he said as he wiped his fingers on his napkin. "The pickle is gone. It no longer exists. It is extinct."

"You mean," said Scout Fred, "that there used to be a creature like this Bigpaw, and now it's extinct?"

"As it happens, my friend, you are exactly right. You see," said the professor, "even the most far-fetched ideas are usually based on something."

"Where does the idea of Bigpaw come from?" said Scout Sister.

"From the giant prehistoric cave bear," said the professor. "A creature that has been extinct for nine million years."

"Wow!" said Scout Brother.

"Gee!" said Scout Fred.

"How about that!" said Scout Lizzy.

The scouts fell silent. They were thinking about what a long time nine million years was.

"This Bigpaw," said Scout Brother. "Was he big?"

"Huge," said the professor.

"Where did he live?" said Scout Sister. "Before he got extinct, that is."

The professor got a far-off look in his eyes. "That's what's so strange about Gran's prediction," said the professor. "He lived right around here."

• Chapter 8 •

A Treasure Beyond Price

The party hadn't been a success for Ralph Ripoff, Bear Country's leading crook and swindler. At least, not so far. Ralph was having a good enough time. He'd passed the time of day with his great and good friend, Mayor Horace J. Honeypot. Ralph's friendship with the mayor had come in handy before and would again. He had been charming to Lady Grizzly. It was all he could do, upon kissing her hand, to keep from taking out his jeweler's glass and inspecting her diamond bracelet.

But being on his good behavior was making Ralph nervous. There wasn't much he could do about it. The food was free, and the balloons weren't worth stealing. Picking pockets was out of the question because Chief Bruno was watching him like a hawk.

After a visit to the food table, Ralph noticed Actual Factual and the Bear Scouts sitting on the oak tree bench. They had their heads together as if they were talking about something really important. Why don't I join them, thought Ralph. I might hear something interesting.

Ralph moved through the shadows and joined Actual Factual and the scouts—on the other side of the bench, of course. What Ralph heard was "interesting" beyond his wildest dreams. This is what he heard:

"Would they be valuable?" said Scout Brother in a hushed voice.

"Valuable?" said Actual Factual.
"They'd be a treasure beyond price. More
precious than diamonds and gold! The find
of the century!"

The words "valuable," "treasure," "diamonds and gold," and "find of the century"
rang in Ralph Ripoff's greedy ears like a
glorious bell. The party hadn't been a fail-

ure after all. It had been a great success. Who needs to pick pockets when you can rip off a fabulous treasure of diamonds and gold? He had to find out where the treasure was hidden, of course. But that shouldn't be hard. Surely there was a map.

Indeed, there *was* a map. A map showing exactly where Actual Factual hoped to find the fossil remains of the giant prehistoric cave bear. That was the treasure the professor and the Bear Scouts had been talking about.

It was all Ralph could do to keep from leaping up and kicking his heels together. But he sat quietly, hardly breathing, until Actual Factual and the scouts got up to leave. He listened hard for more about the treasure. All he heard was something about rock climbing and meeting behind the Bearsonian the next morning.

• Chapter 9 •

"X" Marks the Spot!

"There's still something we don't understand, professor," said Scout Brother. When the Bear Scouts arrived early that morning, the professor had all sorts of rock-climbing gear laid out on the Bear-sonian parking lot.

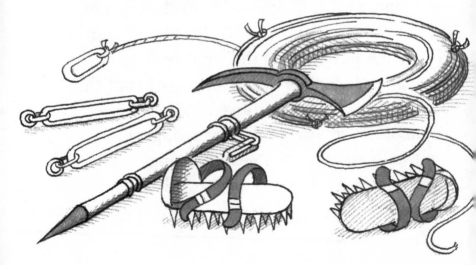

"What's that?" said the professor.

"Well," said Scout Brother. "We thought that the way to find fossils was to dig for them."

"That's usually the case," said the professor.

"But you said we're going fossil hunting in the *mountains*."

"Yes. On Table Rock Mountain, to be exact," said the professor. "Let me explain. It all has to do with changes which have taken place in the earth over millions of years. Many parts of the earth which are now covered by great oceans were once vast deserts. Other parts that are now great mountain ranges used to be swampy lowlands."

"How did all that happen?" said Scout Fred.

"In all kinds of ways," said Actual Factual. "You see, the center of the earth is a great white-hot ball of melted rock.

43

That causes pressure. Sometimes that pressure causes volcanoes, earthquakes. It pushes up great mountains."

Suddenly Scout Sister, who was a bit of a smarty, bent her knees and looked around the parking lot as if she were scared.

"Okay, Sis," said Brother. "What's that about?"

"I'm getting ready to jump out of the way," said Sister, "in case some mountain pushes up through the parking lot."

Her fellow scouts groaned. But the professor laughed. "Anyway," he said. "To make a long story short, my studies show that the lowlands where the giant prehistoric cave bear lived nine million years ago are now none other than the Grizzly Mountains. As a matter of fact, I've pinpointed Table Rock Mountain. Therefore, we shall climb instead of dig."

"I can dig that," said Scout Sister.

This time the professor joined the others in a groan. "And speaking of climbing," he said. "It's time to start your climbing lesson. . . ."

A distance away, high up in a tree, Ralph was watching the lesson through powerful field glasses. It was clear that the treasure he had overheard the professor and the scouts talking about was hidden somewhere in the mountains. But where?

The tree wasn't exactly an easy chair. Ralph had a crick in his neck, an ache in his back, and a cramp in his leg. He was about to climb down from the tree. But something happened that made Ralph forget about the crick, the ache, and the cramp. Actual Factual had stepped into the Bearsonian. A moment later, he came out with a folded piece of paper. He unfolded it and placed it on the ground. It was the map! The Bear Scouts gathered round. Ralph tried hard to read it through the field glasses. But all he could make out was a big "X." The "X" that marked the spot where the treasure was hidden!

Ralph knew what he had to do. His plan called for a very dark night, some skeleton keys, and an after-closing tour of the Bearsonian.

• Chapter 10 •

A Dark and Moonless Night

All was dark in the Bearsonian as Ralph
came out of the bushes and tiptoed up to
the front door. It was a dark and moonless
night. Just the sort of night he had been
waiting for. It hadn't come any too soon.
Ralph had kept watch on the Bear Scouts'
rock-climbing lessons. Those pesky scouts
took to rock climbing like ducks to water.
It was pretty clear that Actual Factual
and the Bear Scouts would be going after
the treasure soon. Ralph was determined
to beat them to it. He had learned quite a
lot about rock climbing from watching the

scouts practice on the small cliff behind the Bearsonian.

He got out his skeleton keys. The third one worked. He slowly pulled the door open, hoping it wouldn't squeak. It didn't. Ralph had been to the Bearsonian a few times and had an idea where the professor's office was. He was pretty sure that was where the map would be.

The Bearsonian, which was kind of spooky even in daylight, was *very* spooky at night. Especially after closing, for somebody who had no business being there. Ralph peered into the darkness as he tiptoed through the museum's great halls. Even machines like old-fashioned steam engines and horseless carriages looked like monsters. And it was really scary moving among the great dinosaur skeletons.

But it was in the Hall of Fame, with its wax statues of famous bears of history, that Ralph got his worst scare. As he moved among the statues of Queen Elizabear, Genghis Bear, and Blackbear the Pirate, a light suddenly flashed up ahead. It was the professor coming out of his office. He was coming right toward Ralph. Think fast, Mr. Ripoff, thought Ralph. He stepped up onto an extra stand and posed like a wax statue. He held his breath until Actual Factual was long past. Then he let it out with a whoosh.

When he was sure it was safe, he stepped down from the stand and moved

to the door of the office. He got out his skeleton keys. But the door wasn't locked. He slipped in, closed the door, and put on the light. The map didn't take much finding. It lay right on Actual Factual's worktable. The "X" that marked the spot almost jumped out at him. How foolish of the professor to leave a valuable treasure map out where anybody could find it. Even better, the spot marked "X" was none other than a certain cave on Table Rock Mountain. Quickly, Ralph made a copy of the map on the professor's copy machine.

Table Rock Mountain was only a couple of miles from Beartown. Ralph knew it well. He'd scramble up old Table Rock Mountain like it was a stepladder. Grab that treasure, and nobody in Bear Country would be the wiser. But Mr. Ralph Ripoff would be much, much richer. Ralph was so pleased with himself that he gave himself a big hug.

• Chapter 11•
The Big Climb

Actual Factual's sciencemobile was bumping and grinding up the back road to Table Rock Mountain. Scout Brother was in the front seat with the Professor, who was driving. Scouts Sister, Fred, and Lizzy were in the backseat, studying the professor's map of the mountains. The sciencemobile was a special van that the professor had fitted out for scientific work. There were picks and shovels for digging, snorkels for underwater study, a minilab for doing tests, and a telescope was built into the roof for studying the skies. And, of course, there was rock-climbing gear for the big climb.

"Professor," said Scout Brother, "I'm still not clear on why you're so sure you're going to find fossils of the prehistoric cave bear on Table Rock Mountain."

"I can't be sure, of course," said the professor, "because there are no sure things in fossil hunting. But to answer your question, I'm very hopeful about the cave marked on the map, because I've been finding shell fossils up here."

"*Shell fossils* in the *mountains?*" said Scout Sister. "That doesn't make sense!"

"It does," said the professor, "if you remember what we were talking about the other day."

"You mean about mountains pushing up out of oceans and stuff?" said Scout Lizzy.

"Exactly," said Actual Factual. "And I didn't just find shell fossils. I've been find-

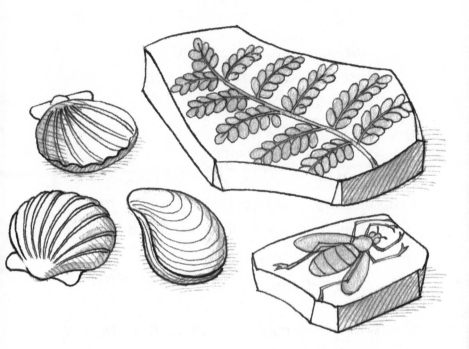

ing fossils of ferns and water bugs. Which
proves that these weren't mountains millions of years ago. This was all low swamp.
Just the sort of place that was home to
shellfish, water bugs, and . . . "

"*Giant prehistoric cave bears!*" said
Scout Sister.

"Perhaps," said Actual Factual.

"Like, wow!" said Scout Sister.

"Outstanding!" said Scout Fred.

"Totally awesome!" said Scout Lizzy.

"I have another question," said Scout Brother.

"Yes," said the professor.

"Why did we take all those rock-climbing lessons," said Scout Brother, "if we're going to *drive* up Table Rock Mountain?"

"You'll be climbing soon enough," said the professor, pulling to a stop on a rocky ledge.

When the scouts climbed out of the sciencemobile, they were startled to see they were already more than halfway to the top of the mountain.

"This is my secret 'backdoor' route. Before I found it, I used to climb the front face of the mountain. It's a very hard climb."

"Look!" shouted Scout Lizzy. "We've got company!" She pointed to some mountain goats on a narrow ledge across the way.

"*We* don't have company," said Actual Factual with a smile. "*They* have company. Amazing animals. Been studying them for years. It's thanks to the mountain goats that we're up here." The Bear Scouts were already wearing their climbing harnesses. The professor was snapping safety lines onto them. "It was during my mountain-goat study that I started finding these strange fossils. It was a pure case of serendipity."

"Seren-whoozy-whatsis?" said Scout Sister.

"Definition please, Fred," said the professor.

"*Serendipity*," said Fred. "Pronounced *ser-en-DIP-i-ty: the finding of something of value by accident.*"

"You mean like if you're picking dandelions and you find a four-leaf clover?"

"Correct," said the professor. "Now, here's our climbing plan: We're not going to climb directly to the cave, which is on the face of the mountain. We're going to climb to Table Rock."

The scouts looked up at the strange rock formation called Table Rock. It was a little scary-looking. The great flat rock was balanced on the mountain's sharp peak.

"Gee, professor," said Scout Brother. "It looks like it might tip over easily."

"No fear of that," said Actual Factual with a chuckle. "It would take a lot more than four Bear Scouts and a skinny professor to tip that rock over. Been balanced up there for millions of years, and it'll stay up there for millions more. In any case, we'll climb to the top. We'll reach the cave by lowering ourselves down the other side. The main cave is just below Table Rock."

The professor began driving spikes for the scouts to hook their safety lines to. He climbed higher and higher, driving spikes

into the mountain as he went. The scouts
followed behind him. As they climbed,
they shifted their safety lines to higher
sets of spikes.

"What about you, professor?" called
Scout Brother. "You don't have any safety
lines!"

"Don't need 'em!" said the professor.
"Forgive me for bragging. But I may just
be the most expert rock climber in Bear
Country."

He certainly seemed to be. He found
footholds and handholds where there
didn't seem to be any. As he climbed up
the mountain, driving spikes as he went,
he seemed as surefooted as his friends the
mountain goats.

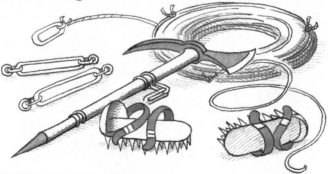

• Chapter 12 •

Oops!

When the Bear Scouts reached the top of Table Rock, the first thing they did was enjoy the view. It was spectacular! As they looked out over the valley, they were filled with pride in what they had done. They could see Beartown far below. They could pick out their homes, Bear Country School, and the Bearsonian. They could even see the smog of Big Bear City in the distance. Though they still hadn't reached their goal—the cave below Table Rock— they had earned the Rock-climbing Merit Badge many times over.

"If only our parents could see us now," said Scout Brother.

"And Gramps and Gran," said Scout Sister.

"And Scout Leader Jane," said Scout Fred.

"And our friends at school," said Scout Lizzy.

"And so they shall!" said Professor Actual Factual. "That's why I brought my camera." He took his camera out of its case and looked into the viewfinder.

"Okay, now. Move closer together," said the professor. He didn't have to ask the Bear Scouts to say "cheese" because they were already grinning like smile buttons. "Closer, so I can get you all in the picture," said the professor, backing up a bit.

Scientists are often said to be absent-minded. But the problem with scientists—and Actual Factual was Bear Country's greatest scientist—is not that they are absentminded. The problem is that they focus so hard on the problem of the moment that they forget to be careful. The professor's problem of the moment was getting all the scouts into the picture. So he kept backing up until he backed right off the edge of Table Rock.

"Professor!" screamed the scouts. Their smiles turned to looks of horror as they rushed to peer over the edge of Table Rock. But instead of seeing the awful thing they expected—the sight of Actual Factual bouncing down the mountainside like a rag doll—they saw something much more shocking. A great hairy arm had reached out and caught the professor in a huge paw. The scouts stared in disbelief as the arm, the paw, and the professor were pulled back into the cave.

As one, the Bear Scouts remembered Gran's prediction.

"Bigpaw!" they said.

• Chapter 13 •

A Chilling Sight

The Bear Scouts were in shock. They wouldn't have been surprised if bits and pieces of the professor had come flying out of the cave.

"Poor Professor Actual Factual!" wailed Scout Lizzy.

"We have to do something!" cried Scout Sister.

"Yes," said Scout Fred. "But what?"

"It's very simple," said Scout Brother. "We have to go down there and rescue him."

"Rescue him?" said Fred. "Did you

see that giant hairy arm?"

"And that paw?" said Lizzy. "It was as big as a Dumpster!"

Scout Brother leaned over the edge of Table Rock. "Here's what we'll do," he said. "There's a ledge off to the side of the cave. We'll take off our safety lines, tie them to one of these rocks, and shinny down to the ledge."

But his fellow scouts just stood there looking scared.

"Look," said Brother. "I know you're scared. We're all scared. We'd be stupid not to be. But being brave when you're scared is what being brave is all about. Now, come on!"

The scouts shinnied down to the ledge.

"So far, so good," said Brother.

"So far, so nothing," said Fred. "Shinny-ing is one thing. Going into that cave is another."

The scouts flattened themselves

against the mountain and inched toward the mouth of the cave.

"We came here looking for cave bear fossils," said Scout Sister. "I'm afraid the only bones we're going to find are the professor's."

"D-don't say things like that," said Scout Lizzy. "It g-gives me the shivers."

"Sorry," said Scout Sister.

They had reached the cave.

"I don't hear any growls or groans," said Fred.

"Or any crunching of bones or grinding of teeth," said Sister.

"Stop *saying* those things!" said Lizzy.

"Sorry," said Sister.

"Come on," said Brother. The scouts followed him into the cave. "Let's just stand here until our eyes get used to the dark. Everybody be quiet and let Lizzy listen."

Lizzy's eyes got used to the dark first. "Ooh!" she said. "Bones!" Sure enough,

there was a scattering of what looked like bones up ahead. Fred investigated.

"Yes!" said Fred. "These could be the fossil bones the professor's looking for!"

"Yuck," said Sister. "Some treasure."

"Hush!" said Lizzy. "I hear voices! I think they're coming from that bend up ahead."

"Follow me and don't make a sound," said Brother.

When they reached the bend they saw something that chilled them to *their* bones. Bigpaw was holding Actual Factual in his big cherry-picker paw. His mouth was wide open and he was looking at the professor as if he were a cherry.

"Here's what we'll do," said Brother in a hushed voice. "Pick up some stones, and on the count of three, start throwing them. Maybe Bigpaw will drop the professor. One, two . . ."

But Brother's voice must not have been as hushed as he thought. Because the professor turned and said, "Dear me! I became so excited about my wonderful discovery that I quite forgot about you. As you can plainly see, our fossil hunt has succeeded beyond my wildest dreams. This cave not only holds the fossil treasure we were seeking, but a far greater treasure: this splendid chap whose measurements I've been taking—teeth, jaws, arm length—that sort of thing. Be a good chap and put me down. I'd like you to meet some very dear friends of mine!"

• Chapter 14 •

A Living Fossil

Bigpaw was much too big to shake hands with the scouts. But the scouts managed to shake one of his giant claws. The great creature didn't have much to say. As each Bear Scout said, "Pleased to meet you, sir," the giant bear smiled a big friendly smile and said, "Hi," in a deep rumbly voice.

The professor kept on making notes. "Teeth, about nine inches long—except for the incisors, which are an amazing sixteen inches long! Gums, healthy. Nose, cool to the touch . . ."

"Sorry to interrupt, professor," said Scout Brother. "But we're confused about all this. I mean, we came up here to look for fossils . . . "

"And we have succeeded!" cried the professor. "We have found some lovely fossil bones for the museum. But even more exciting, we have found a *living* fossil! As far as I know, it's only happened twice in the history of science! There was the okapi, an antelope that was thought to have been extinct for hundreds of years, and the coelacanth, a fish that was thought to have been extinct for millions of years. And now Bigpaw! My friends, I can't tell you how exciting this is. Well, if you'll excuse me, I must get back to my measurements! . . . "

"Couldn't the measurements wait, professor?" said Scout Brother. "There's something we're worried about."

"I suppose they can," said the professor. "What's worrying you?"

"Think back, professor," said Brother. "Think back to when Gran predicted Bigpaw was coming. Remember how scared folks got?"

"Yes, I do remember," said the professor. "They became quite agitated."

"Farmer Ben talked about loading up

his shotgun," said Brother.

"And Mayor Honeypot said just the *mention* of Bigpaw could cause a panic," said Scout Fred.

"You make a very good point," said the professor.

"I mean, *we* know that Bigpaw is sweet and gentle. But he's so frightening-*looking*," said Scout Brother. "When folks see him they'll go nuts! There's no *telling* what they might do."

"You're right," said the professor. "How does this sound as a way of handling the problem? There's a car phone in the sciencemobile. We'll go back down the mountain and call the authorities."

"You mean like Mayor Honeypot?" said Scout Fred.

"Hmm, I think not," said the professor. "Panic is the mayor's middle name. No, Chief Bruno is the bear to talk to. He's a sensible fellow and a friend of mine. But first let me tell Bigpaw we must leave for the moment."

The professor spoke briefly to Bigpaw, then returned to the scouts. "Okay, we're all set. Except that Bigpaw enjoyed meeting you and would like to shake hands again."

So, one by one, the Bear Scouts shook Bigpaw's giant claw again. "Pleased to meet you, Mr. Bigpaw," said each scout.

"Pleased to meet *you*," said Bigpaw, with a shy smile.

• Chapter 15 •

A Hundred Feet Tall
and Eyes of Fire

"Hello, police station. Officer Marguerite speaking."

The police station phone rang often. Most of the calls were about such things as barking dogs, noisy neighbors, and fender-bender accidents. But Officer Marguerite could tell that this call was different.

"Professor Actual Factual, chief. Says he needs to talk to you. Something about preventing a panic."

The chief took the phone. "Chief Bruno

here . . . uh-huh . . . uh-huh. . . . Well, if you think it's important, professor. I've got some things to do, but I'll be there. Just sit tight."

"What is it, chief?" said Officer Marguerite.

"Not something he could talk about over the phone. I've got some business here in town. Then I'll go out and meet him on Mountain Road. Call me on the radio if you need me."

About two miles away, Bear Country's leading crook, swindler, and treasure seeker was slowly working his way up the face of Table Rock Mountain. Ralph didn't go in for fancy harnesses and safety lines. He had a simple and direct approach to mountain climbing. He "borrowed" some tree-climbing tools—foot spikes and a climbing hook—while the lumberjack wasn't looking. His plan was to climb straight up Table Rock Mountain by

driving in the spikes, then pulling himself up with the hook. It was a pretty good
plan, and it might have worked if Ralph

had been in better shape. But he hadn't done any serious climbing since he was a second-story bear back in Big Bear City.

He was getting close to his goal: the cave marked "X." But it was hard going. He'd left a trail of objects all the way down the mountain. The battered brim of his sporty straw hat lay at the foot of the mountain. Its crown was caught on a dwarf pine halfway up. His walking stick had long since clattered down the mountain, frightening the mountain goats. The gold watch he had stolen from a favorite uncle hung on a berry bush.

It had often been said that if Ralph had worked at some honest job half as hard as he did ripping folks off, he'd have been on easy street long ago. But like most folks, he was a creature of habit, and all Ralph's habits were bad. He was close to his goal. But the ledge in front of the cave blocked his view. He couldn't see that what was waiting for him wasn't diamonds and gold, but a very different sort of "treasure."

It was now late afternoon. The sun was setting behind the mountains. Bigpaw had come out on the ledge to enjoy the view. There was a chill in the air. Bigpaw decided to make a fire. He did it the old-fashioned way: by spinning the end of a stick in some dry leaves that were placed in a hollow in a larger piece of wood.

Soon he had a great fire blazing. It sent big sparks up into the air. Bigpaw was at peace. As he sat on a boulder, the fire cast a huge dancing shadow on the mountain-side.

That's what Ralph saw when he finally poked his head over the ledge: a mon-strous, dancing creature with great float-ing sparks for eyes. Ralph was so exhausted from the climb that he couldn't tell where Bigpaw left off and the dancing shadow began.

As he sat on a boulder, the fire cast a huge dancing shadow on the mountainside.

Am I losing my mind? thought Ralph. But while he was wondering about that, he lost something much more important: his grip on the edge of Table Rock Mountain!

It didn't take long for Ralph to bounce, rattle, and roll down the mountain. By the time he reached the bottom, he looked like the loser in a very one-sided fight. What was left of his clothes was in shreds. What was left of his *underwear* was in shreds.

But did Ralph lie there feeling sorry for himself? Well, he did for a moment. But as he lay there in a heap, one thought filled his mind: *I'VE GOT TO WARN THE OTHERS!*

He leaped up and streaked to town. He broke all records for the two-minute mile. *"BIGPAW! BIGPAW!"* he screamed, as he ran through the town. Ralph was a sight. He looked like he'd been chewed up and spit out. A crowd gathered. The crowd

became a mob. Shotguns were loaded. Old
cannons were dragged down from the post
office steps, torches were lit. Soldiers of
the Great Bear War got their uniforms out
of mothballs. Swords were drawn. Pants
were split. The cry "We've got to get him
before he gets us!" went up. The torch-
bearing, gun-toting, cannon-dragging mob
poured out of town and raced toward
Table Rock Mountain.

• Chapter 16 •

A Surging Mob

"They say 'Seeing is believing,' " said Chief Bruno. "But even seeing Bigpaw, it's hard to believe what I see."

The chief had met Actual Factual and the Bear Scouts on Mountain Road. He could see Bigpaw up on his ledge from where they were standing. The chief's car and the sciencemobile were parked side by side.

"From what you're telling me, this Bigpaw—and he sure is big—saved the professor's life," said Chief Bruno.

"He sure did," said Scout Sister.

"Scout's honor," said Scout Brother.

"You did right to call me," said the chief. "The news of Bigpaw *could* cause a panic." The police car radio began to crackle. "Wait a minute. Officer Marguerite is trying to reach me." The chief hurried over to the car.

"Look, professor!" said Scout Lizzy. "Something is happening in Beartown. Some kind of crowd, and they're headed this way."

"I really can't make anything out at that distance," said the professor. "I should have brought my field glasses."

"No need for field glasses, professor," said Scout Brother. "Lizzy has super eyesight. If she says she can see something, you can be sure she sees it."

The chief came back. He'd finished talking on the radio and looked very worried. "That was Officer Marguerite. I'm afraid that what we were worried about has happened. A mob has formed and they're headed this way. She says they're armed. They've got cannons, shotguns, clubs, pitchforks, every sort of weapon they could lay their hands on."

The professor pointed toward Beartown. The mob was closer now. They could be seen clearly in the light of the torches they carried. The chief looked through the field glasses he'd brought from the police car.

"Good grief!" he said. "There's the mayor. He's got his old Bear War uniform on and he's waving a rusty sword!"

"This is awful!" cried Scout Lizzy. "It's like an old black and white movie I saw on TV. It's about this giant gorilla they capture and he gets away and climbs a tall building and they shoot him down with airplanes. It was awful. I cried."

"Don't worry," said the professor. "We'll think of something."

The mob just kept on coming. When they caught sight of Bigpaw up on his ledge, they slowed for a moment. But then they surged forward again, yelling and screaming.

Of course, Bigpaw could see the mob as well as they could see him. While he was a simple fellow, it didn't take him long to figure out that folks with guns and clubs and cannons weren't exactly friendly. He looked around for some way of defending himself.

"Look!" shouted Scout Fred. "Bigpaw's picking up a huge boulder!"

"Can't say as I blame him," said the chief.

"Chief," said the professor. "Do you think those old cannons can reach Bigpaw?"

"Sure," said the chief. "If they don't blow up in the cannoneers' faces."

"Oh, dear! Oh, dear! Oh, dear!" cried Scout Lizzy.

In the excitement nobody noticed that Scouts Brother and Sister had left. They had gotten something out of the police car and were sneaking up the mountain toward Bigpaw.

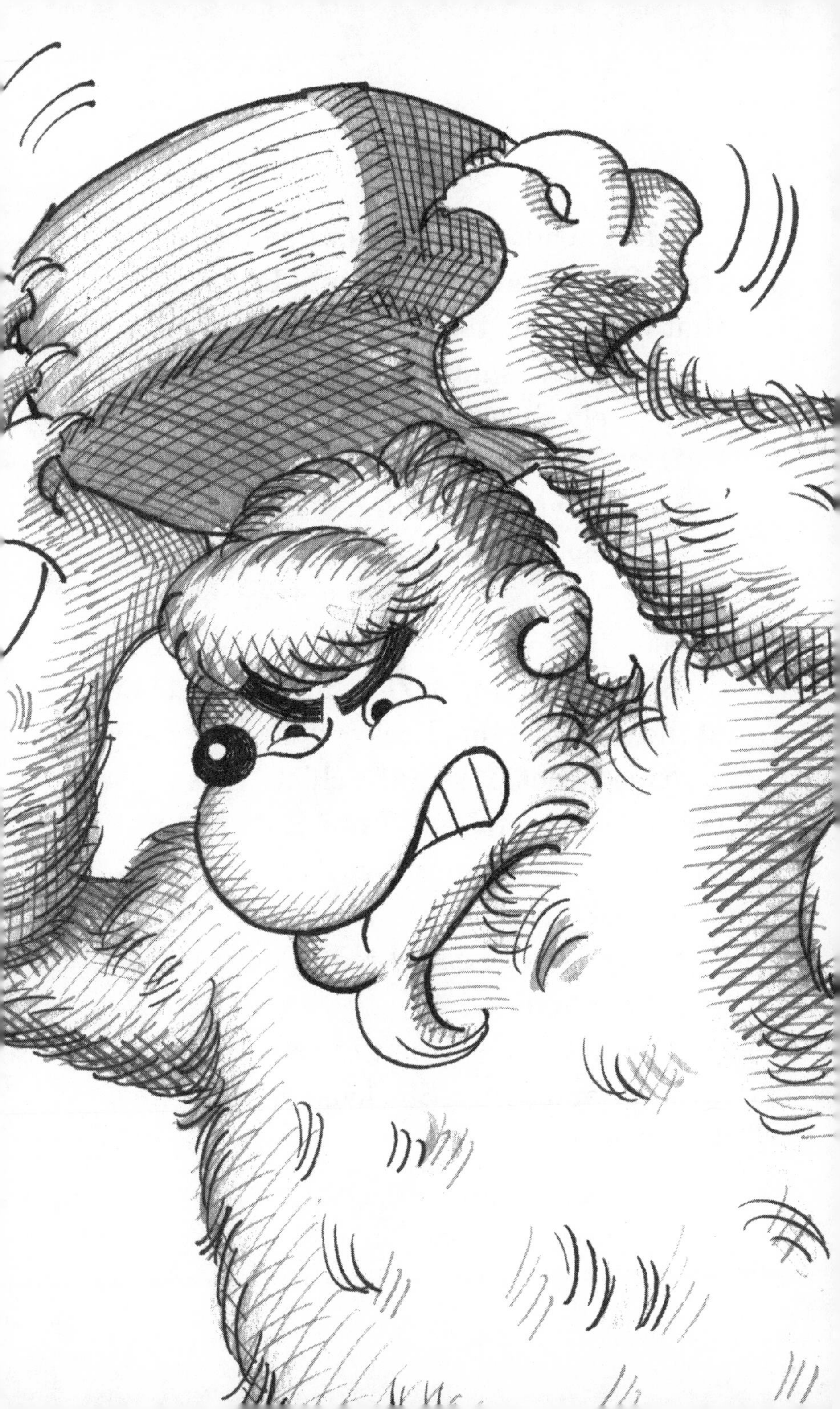

"How about shooting your pistol into the air?" said Actual Factual. "Perhaps that would stop them."

"Too risky," said the chief. "They'd more than likely shoot back."

"Look," said Scout Fred. "Bigpaw's putting down the boulder."

"Oh, my goodness!" cried the professor. "That's just because he's got a much better idea!"

Bigpaw had reached up and taken hold of the edge of Table Rock.

"Good grief!" cried the chief. "He's strong enough to send Table Rock crashing down the mountain. It'll crush the entire mob!"

"Look!" cried Scout Fred. "They're loading the cannons!"

That was when Scout Lizzy missed Brother and Sister. She looked and looked. But they were gone!

• Chapter 17 •

Bigpaw's Our Friend

"There they are!" cried Scout Lizzy. "Climbing up the mountain toward Bigpaw!"

"They've got something with them!" cried Fred.

"Oh, no!" cried the professor.

Brother and Sister had reached a small ledge just below Bigpaw, who was about to tip Table Rock into the valley. It was clear to everyone that Brother and Sister had done a very brave thing. They had placed themselves between Bigpaw and the mob. If Table Rock came tumbling down, it would be good-bye Brother and Sister.

The mob stopped in its tracks. They stopped waving their guns, clubs, and swords. The mob fell silent. In that moment they stopped being a dangerous mob and became a group of individuals worried about the safety of two precious cubs.

What Brother and Sister had taken from the chief's car was a bullhorn. "You must stop!" said Brother, speaking through the bullhorn. "Put down your weapons!"

Then Sister leaned over and spoke into the bullhorn. "Bigpaw's our friend. He's very nice. He saved the professor."

Bigpaw smiled. He stopped rocking
Table Rock. Then he reached down and
scooped Scouts Brother and Sister to
safety.

"...And now he's saved us!" said Sister.
Then she reached up and planted a kiss
on Bigpaw's cheek.

A great cheer went up from the crowd.

They didn't lay their weapons down. They threw them up in the air along with their torches and hats.

Somehow, the sight of a tiny cub planting a kiss on the cheek of that great monster of a bear told the bears of Beartown how foolish they'd been. They had prejudged Bigpaw. They had decided he was bad before they really knew anything about him. It was a moment and a lesson the bears would not soon forget.

And where was Ralph Ripoff when the great trouble he had caused was happening? He was in the Cuts, Scratches, and Bruises ward of Bear Country Hospital. He was checking his new watch against the clock on the wall. He was pleased to find that it was correct.

But Dr. Bearden, who had just examined Ralph, was not pleased to find his watch missing. He was sure he'd had it with him—and, of course, he had.

Save That
Backscratcher

THE Berenstain BEAR SCOUTS

Save That
Backscratcher

by Stan & Jan Berenstain
Illustrated by Michael Berenstain

• Table of Contents •

• Chapter 1 •

A Good Scratch

The Bear Scouts were in high spirits as they tooled along on their way to Scout Leader Jane's. Brother was roaring along on his skateboard. Sister was on her bike. Fred and Lizzy were rollerblading. They had some great ideas for their next merit badge. In fact, they had too many. They'd been arguing about whether to go for the Whitewater Rafting Badge, the Wilderness Camping Badge, or the Scuba Diving Badge. But Scout Leader Jane would help them decide.

"Hey!" called Scout Brother as they

sped along. "We've got plenty of time. Let's stop off at the town square and touch base with Gramps."

The funny thing was that the town "square" was a circle — a traffic circle around a small park. It was a pleasant place where folks liked to pass the time of day. There were benches, some statues, and a great tree that had been there as long as anyone could remember.

GENERAL
GRIZZWELL

The park was set among Beartown's most important buildings: the town hall (the mayor's office was on the second floor), the town library, and the police station and lockup.

But, say, who's that going into the mayor's special entrance? Why, it's none other than Ralph Ripoff, Beartown's leading crook and swindler. Some folks, including Gramps, think that Ralph should be in the lockup instead of making regular visits to see the mayor.

But, be that as it may, it was Gramps's habit to visit the little park at the same time every day. There he would sit on his favorite bench in the shade of the great tree and read the afternoon paper. The tree, a shagbark hickory, was the oldest tree in Bear Country. It was a famous landmark, though nobody thought much about it anymore — except oldsters like Gramps. A brass plate in the ground told the story of "Old Shag." But it was over-grown with weeds.

Gramps truly enjoyed his daily visits to the little park. There wasn't much traffic, and what there was was kind of lazy. The heavy traffic used the main highway and took the bypass around Beartown. Though Gramps was enjoying the quiet and the shade of the great tree, he wasn't enjoying his afternoon paper very much. He was, in fact, finding it quite irritating. Especially the front-page headline, which said, "Mayor Honeypot to Run Unopposed Once Again."

"Humph," grumped Gramps. "High-and-mighty Honeypot! Somebody *should* run against him. Maybe that'd get him down off his high horse."

Gramps went on to read the story that went with the headline. But he was inter-rupted by a loud noise. The noise was a cross between a roar and a rumble, and it

was peppered with bicycle-horn honks and shouts of "Gramps! Gramps! Watch this!" It was the skateboarding, bicycling, rollerblading Bear Scouts. They were bearing down on Old Shag. Gramps picked up his feet as they roared past.

They put on quite a show. They did wheelies and twirlies and jumps and bumps as they circled the huge tree. They nicked its roots in a couple of places and knocked off a piece of its shaggy bark.

Gramps was furious. He leaped up, shouting, "Stop it! Stop it! That's Old Shag you're dealing with! Try to show a little respect!"

The scouts stopped in their tracks. They were puzzled and confused. "Old Shag?" said Sister.

"That's right," said Gramps. "Old Shag's just about the most important tree in Bear Country. It goes back hundreds of years. Old Shag stands for something."

"Gee, we're sorry," said Brother.

"We didn't mean any harm," said Sister.

"I guess not," said Gramps, calming down a bit.

"We were on our way to Scout Leader Jane's. We just thought we'd stop by and say hello," said Fred.

"And show you some of the stunts we can do," said Lizzy.

Gramps picked up the piece of bark and pressed it back into place. "There," he said. "Almost as good as new. Well, it was right thoughtful of you to stop by. I appreciate it. Going to Scout Leader Jane's, you say? Well, be off with you. Give her my regards."

"Will do," said Brother. "Let's go, troop."

As the scouts sped off, Gramps turned

to the tree and said, "They're good cubs,
old friend. But you just can't expect cubs
to understand some things." Then he
leaned his back into the tree and gave
himself a good scratch.

• Chapter 2 •

Shocking News

The Bear Scouts were still bubbling with high spirits and excitement when they arrived at Scout Leader Jane's. But they wouldn't be for long.

It seemed dark in the house after the bright sunlight. So the scouts couldn't see that Jane wasn't her usual smiling self. The scouts were chattering about Bear Scout plans and projects as usual. But Jane stopped them. Their eyes had gotten used to the dark, so they could see that Jane was serious. But they couldn't in a million years have guessed what she was about to say.

"Scouts," she said. "I have an important announcement to make. I have resigned from my Bear Scout duties. I am no longer your scout leader."

The scouts couldn't have been more surprised if Scout Leader Jane had told them she was running for mayor. That was the next thing she told them.

"The reason I am resigning is that I'm running for mayor." With that, she picked up a big roll of paper with a rubber band around it. She removed the rubber band and let it unroll. It was an election poster. It said, "Jane for Mayor."

The scouts understood Jane's words

well enough. But that was all they understood. The idea that Jane would no longer be their leader was shocking and upsetting. It was like having the rug pulled out from under you, like slipping on an icy spot that didn't look icy, like reaching for a step that wasn't there.

It was no wonder the scouts were upset. Jane had been their leader from the beginning. The scouts liked her. They liked her a lot. What they liked most about her was that she didn't fuss at them about every little thing. She trusted them. She let them choose their own merit badges, do their own good deeds. She didn't even seem to mind that they kept their clubhouse a secret.

Jane could read the shock and disappointment in their faces — and the questions. "Of course, you're wondering who your next scout leader will be," she said.

"Well, I'm very glad to tell you that my good friend and fellow teacher, Miss Stickler, has agreed to be your new scout leader."

Jane went on to say a lot more. She said that it had been great being their leader, that she was sure they would do well under their new leader, and that she would miss them. But the Bear Scouts hardly heard her. As it happened, the scouts knew Miss Stickler, though only by reputation. And that reputation was, to put it mildly, a little scary. She taught at the middle school. The rumors about her were that she was . . . well, a stickler: a stickler on grammar, on spelling, on punctuation, on just about everything a teacher can be a stickler about.

The scouts were still lost in thought when they heard Jane say, "Well, are there any questions?" The scouts may have had some, but word had gotten around and the phone started ringing. Jane was kept busy answering it. "Jane for Mayor headquarters, Jane speaking," she said. "I couldn't agree with you more. Our present mayor has been in office much too long . . . I agree about that, too. His relationship with Ralph Ripoff is something we all should be worried about . . . er, would you excuse me for just a moment?" Jane turned to the scouts. "You can let yourselves out, scouts. You're to be at Miss Stickler's tomorrow at three o'clock sharp. Be on time. She's a stickler on punctuality. That's her address on my notepad — and good luck!"

Jane was still on the phone as the scouts let themselves out. Brother was staring at Miss Stickler's address. "Well," he said, "maybe this Miss Stickler won't be as bad as we expect."

Scout Brother was right. Miss Stickler wasn't as bad as they expected. She was much worse.

• Chapter 3 •

Stickler, the Stickler

"That's just gossip and rumor," said Brother.

The Bear Scouts were hurrying to their first meeting with their new scout leader.

"It's not gossip and rumor," said Lizzy. "My cousin Jill goes to middle school, and she says Miss Stickler is the toughest teacher in the whole school. She's a stickler on everything: grammar, spelling, punctuation, manners, posture — *everything!*"

"I heard she gave a cub fifty pages of extra homework for saying 'who' when he should have said 'whom,'" said Fred.

"I heard she kept a cub after school for dotting her *i*'s with little circles," said Sister.

"I heard she made a cub stand in the corner for *slouching*," said Lizzy.

The scouts had reached Miss Stickler's house. "All right! That's enough!" said Brother. "She's going to be our scout leader, and there's nothing we can do about it. So let's try to keep an open mind." He reached up and pressed the doorbell.

"Is that anything like a hole in the head?" said Sister.

The scouts didn't have to wait long. The door popped open before the *ding-dong* inside faded away. And there stood Miss Stickler, the scouts' new leader. She wore harlequin glasses, bangle bracelets, dangle earrings, and a big wide smile with lots of teeth. She didn't look much like a witch, and her house certainly wasn't a candy cottage. But as she stood beaming down at them as if they were chocolate cupcakes with jimmies, they began to feel like Hansel and Gretel.

After giving her watch a quick look, she said, "Names, please!" Then, as the scouts sounded off, she said, "This way, troop!" and led the Bear Scouts into her den.

"Stickler's the name," she said, facing the scouts, "and dealing with cubs is my game. I don't know what you've heard about me. But whatever it is, it's all true. I've got eyes in the back of my head. I can hear the grass grow, and I've got more rules than a dog has fleas. As you may have heard, I'm a stickler about certain things. I'm a stickler about being punctual, for example. You were thirty seconds late. Don't let it happen again. I'm a stickler about posture. You with the glasses. You're slouching," she said, pointing at Fred. He straightened up so hard, his hat fell off.

"I am also, it happens, a stickler about uniforms. So when you put your hat back on, do it properly."

"Properly?" said Fred, picking up his hat.

"And that goes for the rest of you, too!" said Miss Stickler. "Your hats are at more angles than a bunch of Frisbees in the wind." She opened the *Official Bear Scout Handbook*. "'The Bear Scout hat,'" she read, "'shall be worn with the brim straight across and positioned exactly the width of two fingers above the eyebrows.'"

The scouts busied themselves fixing their hats. Especially Scout Lizzy, who was in the habit of wearing hers hanging off the back of her head by the chin strap.

"And while we're on the subject of uniforms," Miss Stickler continued, "your neckerchiefs look like refugees from a rag bin."

The scouts got busy straightening their neckerchiefs.

"And why in the world," said Miss Stickler, pointing at Lizzy, "are your pant legs rolled up?"

"Well," said Lizzy, "we were down by the river because we're planning on going for the Whitewater Rafting Badge. I was wading. So I rolled up my pant legs."

"You can forget about rafting, Lizzy," said Sister, "because Fred and I voted for wilderness camping."

"Forget about wilderness camping," said Brother. "It's the Scuba Diving Badge we're going for."

"Forget all three," said Miss Stickler. "I'm the only one around here whose vote counts, and I vote for the History Merit Badge."

The History Merit Badge? The scouts had never even heard of the History Merit Badge!

• Chapter 4 •

From Bad to Worse

The scouts opened their mouths to protest. But no sound came. It wouldn't have mattered if it had. Because there was no stopping Miss Stickler.

"I happen to be a stickler on history," she said, reopening the *Official Bear Scout Handbook*. "So I was delighted to find this in the appendix. Fred, I understand you read the dictionary just for fun. Define *appendix*."

"*A-p-pendix*," said Fred, a little shaken up. "Pronounced a-PEN-dix: *a short tube in the lower right-hand side of the abdomen*. Its purpose . . ."

A-p-pendix....

"Not *that* appendix," said Miss Stickler. "Huh? Oh," said Fred. "*Appendix: extra material at the end of a book.*"

"Here in the appendix of the *Official Bear*

Scout Handbook — a short tube indeed! — under 'Advanced Merit Badges,'" said Miss Stickler, "are some *wonderful* merit badges. Why, here's the English Usage Merit Badge and the Poetry Merit Badge. And, best of all, the History Merit Badge! It's a wonder to me that you haven't gone for these before instead of all that nonsense about white-water rafting and the like."

The scouts were becoming more and more discouraged. What did English, po-etry, and history have to do with scouting?

Miss Stickler went on for quite a while. "Well," she said finally. "Is all that under-stood? You will submit your ideas on the History Merit Badge as soon as possible. And, oh yes — I'm starting a demerit pro-gram. It will work as follows. Crooked hat, one demerit; sloppy neckerchief, one demerit; pant legs rolled up, two demerits."

There was no question about it. Things were going from bad to worse.

"The meeting is adjourned," said Miss Stickler. "Come! My car's just outside."

The scouts were surprised. "Gee, thanks," said Brother. "But you don't have to drive us home."

"Drive you home?" said Miss Stickler. "Don't be ridiculous. I understand you have a clubhouse. I shall have to inspect it, of course."

"But our clubhouse is a secret!" protested Brother.

"That's right!" said Sister.

"Nobody knows where it is!" said Fred.

"Not even Scout Leader Jane!" said Lizzy.

"*You* know where it is," said Miss Stickler. "Into the car, please."

• Chapter 5 •

Miss Stickler's Way
or the Highway

There was no arguing with Miss Stickler. It was her way or the highway. In this case it was the highway that led past the Bear Scouts' secret chicken coop clubhouse at the far edge of Farmer Ben's farm.

"There it is," said Brother.

It was Miss Stickler's turn to be shocked. "You mean that awful-looking, falling-down mess is your clubhouse?"

Miss Stickler didn't like the Bear Scouts' chicken coop clubhouse one bit. She didn't like the way it looked. She didn't like the way it smelled. (The scouts tried to explain that it had smelled a lot worse before they cleaned it up.) She didn't like it being a secret. She didn't like anything about it. It wasn't long before they were in the car heading back to Miss Stickler's.

"We certainly are going to have to do something about that clubhouse," said Miss Stickler as they drove along. "But don't worry. It's amazing what you can do

with a little paint, some curtains, and a few geraniums. Inside, an air freshener wouldn't hurt at all," she added, wrinkling her nose.

"All right," said Miss Stickler when they got back to her house. "Remember to get back to me with your History Merit Badge ideas as soon as possible."

The scouts headed home in silence.

Sister was the first to speak. "Remember," she said, "when you said Miss Stickler was going to be our scout leader and there was nothing we could do about it? Well, you were wrong. There *is* something we can do about it. We can quit."

Quit. The very word was shocking. It hung in the air as they walked along in silence. It followed them home.

• Chapter 6 •
A Big Decision

"Quit the scouts?" said Gramps. "You can't be the same scouts that came roaring through here full of beans and ready to lick the world the other day."

It was the day after the first meeting with Miss Stickler. The Bear Scouts were sitting with Gramps on his favorite bench in the shade of the most important tree in Bear Country.

The Bear Scouts sighed.

"We're the same scouts, Gramps," said Brother.

The troop had decided to sleep on the

idea of quitting. Now they were doing what they often did when they faced a big decision. They were touching base with Gramps.

"*Those* scouts," said Gramps, "had spirit and grit. Those scouts wouldn't even *think* of quitting just because they got a new scout leader."

Just then a pickup truck stopped at the edge of the park. The driver got out and

walked over to the big tree. He leaned his back into it and gave himself a good scratch. "Phew!" he said. "I really needed that." Then he got back into his truck and drove away.

"Gee, Gramps," said Brother. "What would *you* do if someone took over your secret clubhouse, told you how to wear your hat, and made you go for the History Merit Badge?"

"I'll tell you what I *wouldn't* do," said Gramps. "I wouldn't quit."

"But, Gramps," said Sister. "Scouting isn't about history. It's about whitewater rafting, wilderness camping, and scuba diving. Everybody knows that history is just a lot of boring dates and hard-to-remember names."

"It's funny that you should say that sitting here in this little park in the shade of Old Shag."

"What's the park and some old tree

"This park," said Gramps, "and that 'old tree,' as you call it, are history. History isn't just a bunch of names and dates. History is *what happened!* It's everything that took place to make us what we are today."

That's when Farmer Ben pulled up in his hay wagon. As he climbed down from the wagon, he saw Gramps and the scouts.

"Hi, scouts," he said. "Who was that lady I saw you with at your clubhouse yesterday?"

"That was no lady," said Brother. "That was our new scout leader."

Farmer Ben leaned his back into Old Shag and scratched hard.

"You know, it's kinda funny," he said, as he climbed back onto his wagon. "My back doesn't usually itch that much. But when I see Old Shag, it itches like crazy. Well, see you!" said Ben as he drove away.

"Farmer Ben comes by here fairly often," said Gramps, "sometimes with Mrs. Ben. Yessir, Old Shag means a lot to Bear Country folk. Come with me." Gramps got up from the bench and took Scouts Sister and Lizzy by the hand. Brother and Fred followed along. "You see that statue over there?"

It was a statue of a soldier on a horse. Of course the scouts saw it. They'd seen it many times before. But they had never thought much about it.

"That's General Stonewall Grizzwell," said Gramps. "And that other one is General Ulysses S. Bruin. They were the opposing generals in the Great Bear War."

"Yes," said Fred, who read the encyclopedia, as well as the dictionary, just for fun. "I think I've read about them in the encyclopedia."

"I don't doubt it," said Gramps. "Now, come over here." He led them back to Old Shag. He leaned down and brushed the weeds away from the brass plate at the foot of the tree. "All right," ordered Gramps. "One of you read that out loud. And *then* tell me that history's just a bunch of boring names and dates."

"'Old Shag,'" said Brother, reading aloud. "'Generals Grizzwell and Bruin brought the Great Bear War to an end by signing the peace treaty under this great tree.'

"Wow!" said Brother.

"Gee!" said Sister.

"Very impressive," said Fred.

"Totally awesome," said Lizzy.

"And then," said Gramps, "they sealed the bargain by scratching their backs on

the rough bark of this great shagbark
hickory. As did all the members of their
parties: colonels, majors, captains, right
down to second lieutenants."

"It must have been quite a scene," said
Brother.

"It must have been," said Gramps. "And since then," he continued, "just about every important bear in the history of Bear Country has come here and scratched on Old Shag. Because when you scratch your back on Old Shag, you're scratching it on history."

The scouts could almost see the great historic scene in their mind's eye.

"Scouts," said Gramps. "Aren't your backs beginning to itch just a little?"

"Yes!" said the scouts, almost as one. "They're beginning to itch a lot!"

"Then what are we waiting for?" cried Gramps. "Let's tune in to history! Let's scratch!"

"Ooh! Ah! Oh!" cried the scouts as they scratched and scratched and scratched.

"I wonder," said Scout Brother, when they'd finished scratching, "whether Miss

Stickler would let us do our History Merit Badge about Old Shag."

"Well," said Gramps, "it's certainly something to think about."

• Chapter 7 •

Mr. Mayor, You're in Big Trouble

Perhaps Ralph Ripoff should have been in the town lockup for some of the tricks and swindles he had pulled on his fellow bears. But he wasn't. He was, in fact, in Mayor Honeypot's office, trying to convince him that he was in big trouble.

"There's no doubt about it, Mr. Mayor!" said Ralph. "You're in big trouble."

"Ralph, my fear dellow — er, dear fellow," said the mayor, who sometimes got the fronts and backs of his words mixed up. "I deg to biffer — er, beg to differ. I shall win this election. I shall win it woing agay — er, going away! And the reason is that I am close to the people, the people hold me in great steam — er, great esteem."

"Mr. Mayor," said Ralph. "May I speak frankly?"

"My all beans — er, by all means," said the mayor.

"Mayor," said Ralph, "you haven't been close to the people since you got that mile-long purple limousine you and Mrs. Honeypot ride around in. You haven't been close to the people since Mrs. Honeypot started

MY ALL BEANS —
ER, BY ALL MEANS.

carrying that pink parasol and wearing her glasses on a ribbon."

"Even if that were so," said the mayor, "I won't lose. I *can't* lose, *because nobody is running against me.*"

"But that is not so, Mr. Mayor," said Ralph. "I repeat: not, not, not so."

"*N-n-not so?*" said the mayor.

Ralph picked up a big roll of paper and let it unroll. It was a copy of Jane's election poster. The mayor, who had been standing behind his big, important-looking desk, fell back into his chair. "But . . . but . . . but," he sputtered.

"Jane says you have been in office too long," said Ralph.

"That durts me heeply — er, hurts me deeply," said the mayor.

"She says you have lost touch with the people," said Ralph.

"An arrow heep in my deart — er, deep in my heart!" cried the mayor.

"And that isn't the worst of it," said
Ralph. "She's going to start running TV
commercials tomorrow. Here's one I got
through my spies — er, friends — at the
TV station."

Ralph popped a cassette into the
mayor's VCR. He pushed the power button. Some words came up on the screen.
They said, "Break up the Gang of Two!"

"Tang of Goo — er, Gang of Two," said
the mayor. "Who are they?"

As if in answer, the faces of none other
than the mayor and Ralph Ripoff came up
on the screen. "We give you Honeypot and
Ripoff, the Gang of Two," said the voice on
the TV. It then went on to tell about some
of the crooked schemes Ralph and the

mayor had almost gotten away with.

"But those were *your* ideas, Ralph!" protested the mayor.

"Which I freely admit," said Ralph. "That is why I will bend every effort, go the last mile, to get you reelected. My card, sir."

Mayor Honeypot took the card. It said, "Ralph Ripoff, Election Advisor."

"A little company I have formed," said Ralph.

"What do you advise, Ralph?" said the mayor. "What can I do to get back close to the people?"

"It's too late for that, Mr. Mayor," said Ralph. "You could junk the limo and take away Mrs. Honeypot's parasol. But it wouldn't do any good. No, you've got to do something big, something grand, something that will blow Jane out of the water!"

"What do you suggest?" said the mayor.

Quick as a flash, Ralph reached into an oversized briefcase and took out a folded easel and a flip chart. Then, quicker than a flash, he set up the easel and flip chart. "What I suggest is the Horace J. Honeypot Super-Duper Six-Lane Highway."

That's what it said in big bold letters on the cover of the flip chart.

"Mell me tore — er, tell me more," said the mayor.

• Chapter 8 •

Slogan Time

Meanwhile, down in the park, Gramps and the Bear Scouts were sitting in the shade of Old Shag, eating ice-cream-on-a-stick. Gramps had bought ice cream from the Good Humor Bear. It was to celebrate the troop's decision not to quit scouting. There was no way Miss Stickler or anyone else could drive them out of scouting. Not if they stuck together.

"Save your sticks," said Brother.

"I didn't know you collected ice-cream sticks," said Fred.

"I don't," said Brother, holding out his stick.

The rest of the troop got the message. It was slogan time. Gramps looked on with pride as the scouts crossed sticks and shouted, "One for all, and all for one!"

But the scouts were still worried about Miss Stickler.

"Gramps," said Brother, "I'm not sure Miss Stickler will like the idea of a history project about a . . . well, about a back-scratcher."

"I don't see why not," said Gramps. "Everybody likes a good scratch now and then."

"I don't know about that," said Fred. "I don't think Miss Stickler is the sort of bear who itches."

Just then a van drove up and some election workers got out. They were carrying folding tables and some papers. On the side of the truck it said, "Jane for Mayor!"

The van had a loudspeaker. *"Elect Jane mayor!"* it blared. *"Break up the Gang of Two! Sign our petitions!"*

"I'd know that voice anywhere," said Brother. "It's Miss Stickler!"

Sure enough it was.

"I'd like to meet her," said Gramps. "And now's your chance to talk her into the Old Shag Merit Badge."

"Good idea!" said Brother. "Let's go, scouts."

"Hold it," said Fred. "Don't you think we ought to get our uniform act together first? You know — hats, neckerchiefs."

The scouts fixed themselves up a bit. Then they headed for the van.

"Why, it's my scout troop!" said Miss Stickler. "What are you doing here?"

"Gramps would like to meet you," said Brother.

"And," said Sister, "we'd like to tell you about our History Merit Badge idea."

"Fine with me," said Miss Stickler. She had another worker take over the loud-speaker and went with the scouts.

"Miss Stickler," said Brother, "we'd like you to meet Gramps."

"Delighted, sir," said Miss Stickler.

"And I," said Gramps, "would like you to meet Old Shag."

Miss Stickler was confused. "Old Shag?" she said.

"Yes," said Gramps. "Old Shag is this great tree."

"That's right," said Brother. "We want to do our History Merit Badge about Old Shag."

"Well, it certainly is a handsome tree," said Miss Stickler. "But I am at a loss as to what it has to do with history."

"Why, Old Shag *is* history!" said Gramps. "Here, have a look at this!" He pointed at the brass plate in the ground. Miss Stickler read it.

"Hmm," she said. "I do remember something about this tree. An important treaty was signed under it."

"That's right, ma'am. General Stonewall Grizzwell and Ulysses S. Bruin — those are their statues right over there — signed the treaty ending the Great Bear War under this tree."

The scouts could tell Miss Stickler was impressed.

"And then," continued Gramps, "after they signed the treaty, they sealed the bargain with a good scratch."

"Scratch?" said Miss Stickler.

"That's right," said Gramps. "Because Old Shag is not just a great historic tree. It's a great backscratcher."

"I don't quite understand," said Miss Stickler.

At that moment a big, burly truck driver, who had just parked his six-wheeler, came over.

"'Scuse me, folks," he said. "But I've been on the road for hours and I itch real bad!" Then he leaned his back into Old Shag and scratched like crazy. "Ooh! Ah! Oh! Ooh!" he shouted as he scratched.

"Oh, dear!" said Miss Stickler.

The big truck driver finally stopped. "Terrific scratch," he said. "You ought to try it, lady."

"I, sir," said Miss Stickler, "do not itch."

"It's your funeral," said the truck driver as he left.

"Well!" said Miss Stickler, a little shaken. "I suppose it's all right for you to do your History Merit Badge on this backscra — er, this great historic tree. Now, if you'll excuse me, I must get back to my election duties."

"See, I told you she didn't itch," said Fred.

• Chapter 9 •

Highway Robbery

"It moggles the bind — er, boggles the mind," said Mayor Honeypot.

Ralph's plan was boldness itself. It was to replace the traffic circle and the little park with the Horace J. Honeypot Super-Duper Six-Lane Highway.

"Mr. Mayor," said Ralph. "I am proud to say that this will be the biggest ripoff — er, project — of my career. It will mean jobs, excitement. It will be big news all over Bear Country."

"I can see the upside: jobs, excitement, big news," said the mayor. "But what's the downside?"

"The downside is that if you don't do this," said Ralph, "Jane is going to beat you like a drum."

"I like your idea, Ralph," said the mayor. "I like it a lot. It's a real dum-hinger — er, humdinger! But tell me. Who's going to build this ripoff — er, high-way?"

Ralph whipped out another card. This one said, "Ralph Ripoff, Road Builder."

"Gee, Ralph," said the mayor. "I didn't know you knew anything about building roads."

"Roads are in my blood, Mr. Mayor," said Ralph. "I come from a long line of road builders. My great-uncle, Asphalt Ripoff, built roads all over the world. And his great-uncle, Pothole Ripoff, invented the detour!"

"Won't a six-lane highway through the center of town create a nottlebeck — er, bottleneck?"

"No, sir!" said Ralph. "It's our old-fashioned traffic circle that causes traffic jams."

"Jaffic trams — er, traffic jams," said the mayor. "I've never seen any traffic jams."

"You will, Mr. Mayor. You will." Ralph leaned in close. "My card," he said.

This one said, "Ralph Ripoff, Traffic Jams on Demand."

"Have a look at this." Ralph handed Honeypot a flier. "Hundreds of these will be spread around town."

The flier said, "Present this at the traffic circle and get a free gift."

"What will they get?" said the mayor.

"One of these." Ralph took a balloon out of his pocket and blew it up. It said, "Honk for Honeypot."

"It will be the biggest, noisiest traffic jam Beartown has ever seen," said Ralph.

"I've got to hand it to you," said the mayor. "It looks like you've left no turn unstoned — er, no stone unturned. But tell me. Won't this all cost a lot of money?"

"A *whole* lot of money," said Ralph, leaning in even closer. "My card." This one said, "Ralph Ripoff, Highway Robbery." "That's the beauty part. Please let me explain."

The mayor kept a big jar of coins on his desk. Ralph seized the jar and dumped it right in the middle of the desk. Then he plunged his hand into the pile of coins. As he lifted it out, he let the coins fall back into the pile — *except for the ones that were stuck between his fingers!*

"Do you really think we can get away with — er, convince the voters that the Horace J. Honeypot superhighway is a good thing?"

"We'd better," said Ralph. "Come over here and look out the window, Mr. Mayor."

What the mayor saw made him swallow hard. The little park below was a beehive of "Elect Jane" activity. The Jane for Mayor loudspeaker was going full blast. Folks were lined up around the corner to sign Jane for Mayor petitions.

The mayor sighed. "What will happen to that old tree?" he said.

"Old Shag? It will have to be destroyed, of course," said Ralph. "Well, Mr. Mayor. Is it a 'go'?"

The mayor sighed again. "It's a go," he said.

• Chapter 10 •

This Tree Is Condemned

"Hey! What are you scouts doing down there?"

The scouts looked up to see Officer Marguerite frowning down at them.

"Well?" she said. "I'm waiting for an answer." She was carrying something under her arm.

"We're making a rubbing of this brass plate at the foot of Old Shag," said Brother. He held up the rubbing. It was only half finished.

"Rubbing? Old Shag?" Officer Marguerite leaned forward. "Many's the time

I've scratched my back on this old tree. I didn't even know it had a name. Never noticed this brass plate before, either."

"How about that!" she said, after she read it. "Tell me about this rubbing."

"Well," said Sister, putting the half-finished rubbing back on the plate. "You place the paper so. Then you hold the pencil sort of sideways and rub gently — it has to be gently so you won't break the pencil point or tear the paper."

"You could use a crayon," said Fred. "Or an art pencil with big thick lead. It tells how to do it in the *Official Bear Scout Handbook*."

Sister was still at work.

"This rubbing," said Officer Marguerite. "What's it for?"

"It's for a Bear Scout merit badge — a *History* Merit Badge," said Fred. "You see, we have this new scout leader, Miss Stickler, and . . ."

"Miss Stickler?" said Marguerite. "I had her in middle school. Talk about tough. She caught me chewing gum once. Made me chew that same piece of gum for a week. My jaws are *still* tired. History, you say. What are you going to do with the rubbing?"

"Our History Merit Badge project is going to be a big album," said Fred. "It's going to have all kinds of history stuff in it: this rubbing, photographs, maps, old letters, whatever."

"There's plenty of history around here," said Marguerite. "There's no doubt about that. See that statue over there? That's General Stonewall Grizzwell. He was my great-grandfather on my mother's side. My mother's a Grizzwell. His name's right there in the old Grizzwell family Bible."

"Do you think maybe we could make a copy of the page with his name?"

"Don't see why not," said Marguerite.

"I'm a Bruin," said Lizzy. "My dad says that other general, Ulysses S. Bruin, was my great-great-grandfather."

"How about that," said Officer Marguerite, looking at the little park with all its history. "Just think. Your great-great and my great signed a big peace treaty under this big old tree."

"And then they scratched their backs on it to seal the bargain," said Fred.

"So they say. So they say," said Marguerite. She looked around the little park again. "You know something?" she said. "I'm glad you're doing this. That album will be a good thing to have when this old tree is gone. What did you say its name was?"

"Old Shag," said Brother. "What do you mean, 'gone'?"

"Just what I said," said Marguerite. "This tree is condemned." With that, she hung the sign she'd been carrying on Old Shag. The sign said, "This tree is condemned — by order of Horace J. Honeypot, Mayor."

"Condemned?" said Sister. "What's that mean?"

"It means they're going to take it down and grind it up into sawdust."

"What?" cried the scouts.

"Yep. Tomorrow afternoon at exactly two o'clock," said Marguerite. "The mayor's going to be here, Mrs. Honeypot, TV cameras, the works. Going to be a big deal. Mayor's going to cut a ribbon for the new highway. Well, see ya."

The Bear Scouts were stunned. They could almost hear the growl of the chainsaw as it cut down Old Shag and the awful roar of the chipping machine as it ground Old Shag into sawdust.

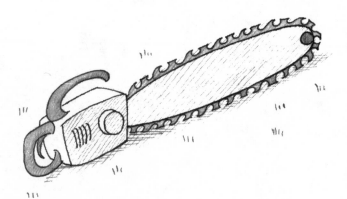

• Chapter 11 •

Emergency Meeting

"This emergency meeting of the Bear Scout troop will come to order," said Miss Stickler. "Be it noted that Gramps, a friend of scouting, is also . . ."

"Never mind all that," said Gramps, breaking in. "Let's get down to business! They're gonna murder Old Shag, and we gotta stop 'em!"

"Calm down, Gramps," said Brother. "Miss Stickler is on *our* side."

"Thank you, Brother," said Miss Stickler. "Gramps, I am a stickler for rules. I insist that this meeting be run by the rules in the *Official Bear Scout Handbook*. The floor is now open for suggestions as to how to save Old Shag."

Brother raised his hand.

"Brother has the floor," said Miss Stickler. But Gramps broke in again.

"Never mind all this fancy-pants floor nonsense," said Gramps. "You want a suggestion? I'll give you a suggestion! I suggest that the first thing we gotta do is run that no-account crook, Ralph Ripoff, out of town! He's the one at the bottom of all this superhighway nonsense! Horace Honeypot hasn't got the *brains* to . . ."

"GRAMPS, IF YOU PLEASE!" said Miss Stickler.

"Please calm down, Gramps," said Sister. "We know you're upset. But shouting at Miss Stickler isn't going to help Old Shag."

"Thank you, Sister," said Miss Stickler. "As I was saying, Brother has the floor."

"Here's what I was thinking," said Brother. "Aren't there laws protecting things that are part of history? Maybe there's some law that'll protect Old Shag."

"It's a good thought," said Miss Stickler. "I checked and, yes, there is such a law. It's meant to protect buildings. As far as I could find out, it does not protect trees. Not even a tree as important as Old Shag." Lizzy raised her hand. "Yes, Lizzy. You have the floor."

"What about all the animals who live in Old Shag?" said Lizzy. "There must be hundreds of squirrels, birds, and insects who live in Old Shag. They'll all be home-less if . . ."

"I don't believe this!" cried Gramps. "They're gonna grind Old Shag into saw-dust and we're still sittin' here talkin' about squirrels and birds and bugs. Well, count me out! I'm leavin'! I know Horace Honeypot! Before he got so high-and-

mighty, we used to be friends. Me and
Gran and him and Hannah used to double-
date. We used to go fishing together. We
used to scratch our backs together. You
can go on with your meeting. But I'm leaving. I'm going out to his house and give

him a good talking-to. And if that doesn't work, I'm gonna give him a good shaking. And if that doesn't work, I'm gonna give him one of these!" Gramps held up a bony fist.

Gramps was almost out the door when Brother grabbed him. "Wait, Gramps," said Brother. "I may have an idea. You say you and the mayor were friends?"

"We were buddies," said Gramps.

"And you used to scratch your backs together on Old Shag?" said Brother.

"Sure. Where else?" said Gramps. "But that was a long time ago."

The scouts, Gramps, and Miss Stickler listened as Brother told them his idea.

"Hmm," said Gramps.

"Hmm," said Sister.

"Hmm," said Fred.

"Hmm," said Lizzy.

"You know something?" said Miss Stickler. "It just might work."

• Chapter 12 •

Ooh! Ah! Oh! Ah!

All was in readiness for the big ribbon-
cutting. Gramps, Miss Stickler, and the
Bear Scouts got to the traffic circle park
with time to spare. At first it looked as

though they might not get in. The park
was roped off so that there was only one
entrance. And you had to have tickets.
That was something they hadn't counted
on. If they didn't get in, they couldn't save
Old Shag. They could see the chainsaw
crew and the chipping machine at the
edge of the park.

The scouts had seen chipping machines in action. Farmer Ben had one. He used it when he cleared scrub. It ate whole trees the way rats eat cheese.

Luckily, the Bear Scouts' friend Officer Marguerite was taking tickets. She let them in without any. She certainly had been right when she said this was going to be a big deal. A crowd was beginning to gather in the park. An even bigger crowd was gathering in the grandstands placed around the traffic circle. There were TV cameras all over the place. There was even a TV remote truck from Big Bear City.

There was a big yellow ribbon stretched across the park. This was where the highway was going to go. The mayor would cut the ribbon. Then the crowd would cheer for his reelection. At least, that was what was supposed to happen.

Gramps, Miss Stickler, and the scouts didn't stay together. As they moved among the crowd, they were careful to stay out of the way of Ralph Ripoff. Ralph was handing out Honeypot for Mayor signs. He didn't know Miss Stickler. But he knew Gramps and the cubs all too well.

They couldn't be sure their plan would work. But to carry it out, they would have to be close to Old Shag when the mayor made his speech and cut the ribbon. They worked their way closer and closer. The "condemned" sign was still hanging on the grand old tree. They could hear the sound of the chainsaws being tested. They could see the big orange chipper waiting for its dinner.

The crowd stirred. The mayor and Mrs. Honeypot were arriving in the purple limousine. The TV cameras turned toward them. Ralph held up a big applause sign. There was some applause. Mrs. Honeypot was carrying a pink parasol and wearing her glasses on a ribbon. There was a

speaker's platform with a microphone. The Honeypots mounted the platform. The mayor came to the microphone. He raised his arms to the crowd. There was a little more applause.

The chainsaws were at the ready. The mayor was about to speak, but before he could start, six members of the crowd sprang into action. They were Gramps, Miss Stickler, and the scouts, of course. Before anyone could stop them, they had thrown their backs against Old Shag. With arms linked, they made a chain around the great tree and began to chant, "Save Old Shag! Save Old Shag! Save Old Shag!"

All the TV cameras turned toward them.

"What in the world do you think you're doing?" shouted the mayor.

"We're calling you home, Horace!" cried Gramps. "We're calling you back to yourself, old friend!"

The mayor recognized Gramps. "Look, Hannah," said the mayor. "It's our old friend Ernest!"

By this time the crowd had taken up the cry. "Save Old Shag! Save Old Shag!"

"I didn't know your name was Ernest," said Brother.

"Have them arrested!" said Mrs. Honeypot.

"Doesn't your back itch just a little?" called Gramps, as he scratched his back on Old Shag. "Oh, that feels good!" cried Gramps. "Doesn't it itch *just a little,* Horace?"

"Why, yes." The mayor reached over his shoulder to scratch. "Why, yes, it does. Just a little."

"Then, come on down!" cried Gramps.

The mayor leaped down from the platform and threw his back against Old Shag. "Yes! Yes!" he cried. "It itches a lot! Yes! Yes! Ooh! Ah! Yiii! Oh! Ah! Ooh!"

The crowd stopped chanting and began to cheer the mayor. This time, for real.

"Come, Hannah. There's nothing like it! Ooh! Ah!" cried the mayor.

Mrs. Honeypot hesitated for a moment. But then she threw away her parasol, leaped from the platform, and put *her* back into it. "Mmm! Ah! Oh! Oh!"

The cameras rolled. The crowd roared. A good scratch was had by all. Even Miss Stickler sneaked a bit of a scratch when she thought no one was looking.

Finally, the mayor stopped scratching.

He mounted the platform, raised his arms for quiet, and said, "The Horace J. Honeypot Super-Duper Six-Lane Highway is hereby cancelled!"

The roar of the crowd was tremendous.

They had done it. Their plan had worked. Old Shag was saved.

• Chapter 13 •

Jane's Return

As it turned out, Mayor Honeypot won the election. It was close. But Honeypot won. Some said he won because he had so many relatives and some of them may have voted twice. But Gramps didn't agree with that. Gramps thought it was because the mayor had gotten back to his roots,

because he'd gotten down off his high horse and scratched his back. "Folks identify with that," said Gramps. "Everybody needs a good scratch now and then. Even folks who 'don't itch,'" he added with a wink.

It wasn't easy for Jane, of course. Nobody likes to lose. But she was glad she had run. At least she had broken up the Gang of Two. It was reported that when last seen, Ralph Ripoff was out on the main highway selling balloons.

Candidate Jane was also very glad to get back to being Scout Leader Jane. The Bear Scouts were *very* glad to have her back. Not that they didn't appreciate Miss Stickler. She was tough. But they had learned a lot from her — especially about history. They were proud to have earned the History Merit Badge. They were very proud that the album they had made — it was called "Old Shag: A History" — had

been put in the Beartown Library for all
to see.

The Bear Scouts were at their first
meeting since Scout Leader Jane's return.

"Jane," said Brother, "we've been having
an argument about which merit badge to
go for next: the Whitewater Badge, the

93

Wilderness Badge, or the Scuba Diving Badge."

"I'm not in favor of any of those," said Jane. "The badge I want to go for is the 'Just Relax and Have Fun Badge'!"

"But there is no such badge," said Sister.

"There is now," said Jane with a grin.

So that's what the scouts did. They just relaxed and had fun for a while. They skateboarded. They bicycled. They rollerbladed. And every so often, they stopped for a good scratch.